"Garrett."

He turned his head, and looked from Emma's face to the hand she offered. For the first time, Garrett saw something in her eyes that translated to hope.

Enclosing her small hand in his, he brought it to his lips. "You'll stay?"

Slowly she searched his face. "I'll stay."

For an instant, their eyes met and held, and then she moved into his arms.

"We're going to work this out," Garrett said, fighting the welling of emotion so strong, it stung his eyes. "I want you back. You. The woman I married."

"What if that woman no longer knows what she wants? What if she's gone?"

Garrett looked into Emma's soulful brown eyes, and then hugged her closer. "Then we'll find her. Together."

Dear Reader,

The perfect treat for cool autumn days are nights curled up with a warm, toasty Silhouette Desire novel!

So, be prepared to get swept away by superstar Rebecca Brandewyne's MAN OF THE MONTH, *The Lioness Tamer,* a story of a magnetic corporate giant who takes on a *real* challenge—taming a wild virginal beauty. THE RULEBREAKERS, talented author Leanne Banks's miniseries about three undeniably sexy hunks—a millionaire, a bad boy, a protector—continues with *The Lone Rider Takes a Bride,* when an irresistible rebel introduces passion to a straight-and-narrow lady…and she unexpectedly introduces him to everlasting love. *The Paternity Factor* by Caroline Cross tells the poignant story of a woman who proves her secret love for a brooding man by caring for the baby she *thinks* is his.

Also this month, Desire launches OUTLAW HEARTS, a brand-new miniseries by Cindy Gerard about strong-minded outlaw brothers who can't stop love from stealing their own hearts, in *The Outlaw's Wife.* Maureen Child's gripping miniseries, THE BACHELOR BATTALION, brings readers another sensual, emotional read with *The Non-Commissioned Baby.* And Silhouette has discovered another fantastic talent in debut author Shirley Rogers, one of our WOMEN TO WATCH, with her adorable *Cowboys, Babies and Shotgun Vows.*

Once again, Silhouette Desire offers unforgettable romance by some of the most beloved and gifted authors in the genre. Don't forget to come back next month for more happily-ever-afters!

Regards,

Joan Marlow Golan
Senior Editor, Silhouette Desire

Please address questions and book requests to:
Silhouette Reader Service
U.S.: 3010 Walden Ave., P.O. Box 1325, Buffalo, NY 14269
Canadian: P.O. Box 609, Fort Erie, Ont. L2A 5X3

CINDY GERARD
THE OUTLAW'S WIFE

SILHOUETTE *Desire*®
Published by Silhouette Books
America's Publisher of Contemporary Romance

This book is dedicated to Bobbie McLane and
Donna Young, of Basically Books.
Romance has never had better friends.

Thanks for the confidence you instill, the enthusiasm you
dish out, and for selling the heck out of my books!

 SILHOUETTE BOOKS

ISBN 0-373-76175-9

THE OUTLAW'S WIFE

Copyright © 1998 by Cindy Gerard

Books by Cindy Gerard

Silhouette Desire

The Cowboy Takes a Lady #957
Lucas: The Loner #975
***The Bride Wore Blue* #1012
***A Bride for Abel Greene* #1052
***A Bride for Crimson Falls* #1076
‡*The Outlaw's Wife* #1175

**Northern Lights Brides
‡Outlaw Hearts

CINDY GERARD

If asked "What's your idea of heaven?" Cindy Gerard would say a warm sun, a cool breeze, pan pizza and a good book. If she had to settle for one of the four, she'd opt for the book, with the pizza running a close second. Inspired by the pleasure she's received from the books she's read and her longtime affair with her husband, Tom, Cindy now creates her own warm, evocative stories about compelling characters and complex relationships.

All that reading must have paid off, because since winning the Waldenbooks Award for Bestselling Series Romance for a First-Time Author, Cindy has gone on to win the prestigious Colorado Romance Writers' Award of Excellence, *Romantic Times* W.I.S.H. awards, Career Achievement and Reviewer's Choice nominations and the Romance Writers of America's RITA nomination for Best Short Contemporary Romance.

Dear Reader,

One of the best things about writing for Silhouette
Desire is the license I'm granted when creating my story
lines. My new miniseries, OUTLAW HEARTS, is a
perfect example of that freedom. Despite the potential
for controversy, in this first book, *The Outlaw's Wife*,
I've been given the latitude to tell a story about a
married couple struggling with some very real problems
in some very extreme ways.

While many will applaud, some may not sanction the
events that transpire between Garrett and Emma James.
It is my hope, however, that all will be moved by this
exploration of the fallibility and the frailty of the human
condition and the resultant misunderstandings the
silence of assumption can breed.

Hang on for a ride filled with tears, laughter and sensual
exploration as Garrett and Emma make mistakes and
discoveries in their search for the courage to hold on to
a marriage that love alone can't save.

All my best to you,

Cindy Gerard

Prologue

She'd become his wife ten years ago; she'd become his life even before that. On the first day that Mississippi's own sloe-eyed Emma DuPree had sashayed her transplanted Southern self into Jackson High's hallowed halls, Wyoming-born and Western-wild Garrett James had flat-out fallen in love.

She'd been all of sixteen. He'd been almost a man. Heavy snows had been falling that January afternoon when they'd collided head-on at the seventh-hour study hall door. Embarrassed, she'd smiled shyly up at him over the bundle of text books tumbling from her arms—and opened a window of sultry Southern heat onto a cold Jackson Hole winter.

From the beginning he'd been lost—in her slim curves, her shining chestnut hair and her unconsciously sexy drawl. She'd turned his eighteen-year-old legs to noodles and his awakening heart to mush. All these years later she still did.

That's why it hurt so much.

He was losing her. After all those years of loving her, after counting on forever, he was losing her. And, God help him, he didn't know how to set things right.

As he walked his mother down the aisle of the church, he sought Emma out through the gathered congregation. Their eyes met. In that brief moment of contact before she looked away, he felt the cutting absence of both the softness in her cinnamon brown eyes and the warmth of her giving heart.

With concentrated effort he stalled the gnawing ache of loss. This was not the day, now was not the time, to wallow in the mess of his marriage. This day belonged to another woman in his life. For her sake he'd make sure it was a celebration she'd always remember.

With pride and admiration he walked his mother toward the man who would make her his wife.

Fifteen years had passed since Garrett and his brothers had lost their father and Maya James had buried her husband. No one could replace Jonathan James in his sons' eyes, but Logan Bradford offered their mother a chance at happiness again. For that, all three brothers were grateful.

Not that Bradford would have been swayed if they hadn't sanctioned the marriage. Either he hadn't heard or didn't care that, like their distant and notorious outlaw ancestors, they were a formidable and imposing lot—and that nobody messed with the James boys.

Garrett conceded that their reputations were well earned. As kids they'd been hell-raisers. As men they still were, to some folks' way of thinking.

Jonathan James's death had left a young widow with

a heartful of grief and three confused and angry young sons. The rebellions had been inevitable. Despite them Maya had managed to keep Jonathan's construction business going and raise her boys right, in all ways that counted. To a man, they were ethically solid and morally strong—yet as different as earth and sky.

As the eldest, Garrett was standing in as father of the bride. As requested by the groom, he was also doubling as best man. *Best man.* In more ways than one, he knew that was how his younger brothers regarded him. The irony was as twisted as it was excessive. He alone knew the reason why every day of his life he tried not to let them down. He alone lived with a guilt and a sense of responsibility that was his alone to bear—and made him far from the best of these men.

Bradford's presence in his mother's life would ease the responsibilities he'd taken upon himself at sixteen. Nothing, however, would minimize the culpability he felt over his father's death.

While he was alone with his guilt, in all else the brothers were solidarity personified. Cross one, you crossed the whole clan—and they were not a forgiving lot.

Not that they looked so tough today, Garrett thought as Clay and Jesse, standing by the front pew, watched their mother approach on Garrett's arm. Their expressions were indulgent, their bold blue eyes soft in contrast to the crisp black tuxedos they wore.

Though he was taller than the other two, who both pushed six feet, Garrett had often been told they all exemplified the best of their parent's blood. Like his brothers, Garrett's dark good looks reflected a rich, mixed lineage of melting pot and native American on his father's side. The European ancestry brought to them by their mother was responsible for a subtly aristocratic bone structure and the unusual quicksilver blue of their eyes. Bred into them just as definitively was their rock-solid work ethics and family values.

Family values. Of the three of them, Garrett held that concept at the highest premium. Involuntarily his gaze strayed back to Emma. Standing by the front pew, she held their eight-year-old daughter's hand in hers. To look at them, no one would guess that the family he valued above all else was in danger of falling apart.

The slight pressure of his mother's fingers on his arm eased his attention back to her. She shot him a sassy wink. He squeezed the small but strong hand tucked in the crook of his elbow, gave up a small grin and placed his problems on hold. Then he let his gaze drift back to his brothers.

What a crew. Clay, at thirty-one and two years younger than Garrett, stood second in line and in age. He was also Garrett's business partner. Clay had joined him in their father's construction company when their mother had gladly relinquished control several years ago.

If Garrett didn't miss his guess, Clay was nursing a notion to settle down. And good luck, ladies, he thought with mild amusement. Many a determined mover and shaker had set her mind to convincing Clay James she was the one he needed to settle down with. Clay didn't want a mover and a shaker. He wanted a down-home girl. One who'd be satisfied with hearth and home, raising babies and taking care of him. He wanted a woman who would put him before her career—a rare if not extinct species, Garrett thought with a tilt of his lips, and wondered if either Clay or Maddie Brannigan, Emma's unorthodox and fiery friend, would admit to the fire shooting like sparks from a welder between them.

Garrett's smile grew bigger when he looked at the fidgeting man next in line. He loved and respected both his brothers but he'd always had a soft spot for Jesse.

At twenty-eight Jesse was the youngest of the three of them, and the closest to living up to his outlaw name. Since the day he'd been born, in the middle of a Wyoming blizzard, he'd cheerfully and with undisciplined enthusiasm, earned his "hell-raiser" reputation.

More comfortable wearing denim and dust, Jesse tugged discreetly at the collar of his starched white shirt, then clasped his calloused hands loosely in front of him. Unlike Clay, who was selective, Jesse was generous with his affection for women. He loved them all. All kinds. All models. All ways.

"Mind you, Emma's one very special lady," Jesse had conceded to Garrett several years ago over a backyard barbecue and a bottle of beer, "but for the life of me, I can't figure why any man with both feet in the stirrups would want to settle for one flower when there're fields of wild blossoms out there just waiting to be picked."

Jesse's broad shoulders, twin dimples and bad-boy swagger had landed him in the middle of those colorful flower beds on a regular basis. His life on the pro rodeo circuit offered too many opportunities to keep his ways and his women just the way they were—wild, reckless and as unpredictable as the bulls he rode—unlike Logan Bradford, Garrett reflected, and diverted his attention to the man who would now share his mother's life.

Bradford hadn't gotten where he was today—the CEO of a high-profile, high-profit marketing firm here in Jackson Hole, Wyoming—by being careless. He had

both the savvy and the intelligence to realize he would
face a mob of James boys taking the law in their own
hands if he didn't treat their mother with all the respect
and devotion she deserved. Garrett had every confidence that he would.

Maya gave Garrett's arm a reassuring squeeze as they
reached the altar. After placing a soft kiss on her cheek,
he relinquished her hand.

Logan's gaze encompassed Maya's two youngest
sons, then landed on Garrett. *She's not yours to take
care of anymore, gentlemen.* It was with both relief and
satisfaction that Garrett acknowledged Logan's unspo-
ken message. The glow of happiness on his mother's
face gave him the final assurance he needed.

He stepped back in line with his brothers and in a
moment that was brutally stunning for its clarity, acknowledged the demise of his own happiness with
Emma.

He dealt with the unexpected punch of that sobering
thought by trying to suppress it. It didn't work. His
attention strayed back to his wife. Grim-mouthed, he
studied the face he loved, the unmistakable shades of
unhappiness dulling her eyes. And he wondered, as he
had for months, what he could do to make things right
between them again.

Tomorrow, he told himself resolutely as the day wore
on and he accepted the congratulations of the well-
wishers at the reception, tomorrow he'd take some time
away from work that he'd been promising her he'd take.
He'd set his priorities and his house back in order. He'd
force himself to deal with the defeating knowledge that
something was wrong with his marriage. Something he
hadn't wanted to identify or name. Something that kept
him awake nights wondering where to begin the search
for the love he and Emma seemed to have lost.

One

May, two months later.

Despite Viola DuPree's hypochondriac tendencies, Emma James loved and worried about her mother. Until today, however, Emma had never thought she'd be thanking the medical profession for catering to Viola's "Valium deficiency" by keeping her well stocked with the tranquilizing medication.

But then, she'd never thought she would catch Garrett with another woman, either.

With a cautious glance over her shoulder to make sure her mother was still asleep, Emma opened the medicine cabinet in Viola's bathroom. Despite her shaking hands, she found the bottle she wanted and managed to tip several tablets into her palm. Swallowing back a fresh wave of pain and staunchly shoving aside the guilt over what she was about to do, she replaced the bottle on the shelf. Then, tiptoeing past the bedroom where Viola indulged in her afternoon nap, Emma slipped silently out of her mother's house and eased into her car.

She tried not to think about it, but between stops at the butcher's, then the farmer's market, the picture of Garrett and that blonde kept flickering through her mind like a bad movie. Nausea accompanied every replay. Acute, absolute loss followed.

Garrett hadn't seen her. And Emma hadn't had the courage to confront them. Not in front of all those people. Not in the midst of a brilliant May afternoon cluttered with birdsong and the sweet scent of flowers—and her husband and the father of her child in the arms of another woman.

She bit back tears and turned left on Elm. It all made sense now. Why hadn't she seen it coming? It wasn't as though she hadn't had plenty of warning. All those late-night "meetings." The constant extra hours he'd been putting in lately. Those sudden, unplanned overnighters. She should have realized. The way he'd closed himself off from her the past several months hadn't translated to fatigue as she had thought. It translated to boredom—with her and with their marriage.

What a fool. What a simpering, gullible fool she'd been. Tears stung then blurred her vision. She swiped them angrily away. Her mother had warned her. For once, Viola DuPree's erratic ramblings had been sound. She'd told Emma from the beginning that tangling with Garrett James would end in a broken heart.

Broken. Battered. Bleeding.

Sheer will got her home and into the house. Blind courage got her through the hours until Garrett was due home.

Garrett had always said he liked her in silk. When he walked through the front door several hours later, she was dripping in it—a soft, watery blue tank top, over-size and cut low to show a hint of cleavage, the hem long and flowing over matching pajama pants.

His gaze drifted with interest over her body, lingering on her breasts, unencumbered beneath the revealing fabric, before it shifted slowly to her long chestnut hair, shining and loose and falling seductively over one eye.

He arched a dark brow, took in the dining room table, set with candles and crystal and a deep burgundy wine already poured and brought to room temperature the way he liked it.

"You've been busy." He set a briefcase full of paper on the floor. "School let out early today?"

She made herself hold on to a smile—it was a trick she'd perfected during her six years as a teacher. Third graders could try the patience of a saint. She wasn't feeling saintly now. She was feeling wronged. She was feeling raw.

"Broken water main," she said, her voice lapsing into what Garrett called her Mississippi memory. She'd lost most of her drawl over the years. Only when she was upset did it make an appearance these days. Hoping he hadn't noticed, she concentrated on keeping it under wraps. "Classes were canceled. I worked on tomorrow's lesson plans at home most of the day."

"Looks like you worked on something else, too." His gaze, glittering and sparked with interest, danced to the table then back to her. "Are we celebrating something?"

Yes, she thought, We're celebrating. We're celebrating the demise of my stupidity.

She tried and failed to push from her mind the picture

of Garrett and his lover cozied up together. They'd been so full of secret smiles as they'd leaned across the table at the sidewalk café, eyes only for each other.

With a controlling swallow, she blinked back the image of the woman's long, elegant fingers. Tipped with perfectly manicured scarlet nails, those fingers, she knew, had stroked through Garrett's thick, luxuriant hair with intimate and possessive familiarity.

Emma had always loved his hair. Black. Lush. Hers. Ten years ago she'd made him promise that once they were married, he wouldn't let anyone but her and his barber ever touch his hair again.

It had been a young lover's promise. Playful. Silly. Romantic. A metaphor for the faith they'd placed in each other. Today she'd watched him break that promise. It was the thought of all the other promises he'd broken that she couldn't bear.

She made herself respond to the question in his eyes.

"When you called to say you'd be late, I figured you'd had another tough day." It was a struggle to keep her voice calm, her eyes inviting instead of accusatory. "I thought an intimate dinner for two would be in order."

He smiled. A crooked, full-of-himself smile. It was the same smile that had drawn her to him in the beginning. The same smile that had made her heart trip, her pulse race, and prompted a fervent, passionate *yes* when he'd asked her to marry him ten years ago.

It was the same smile he'd given to the blonde today.

The pain clutched hard and twisted.

"Sounds nice," he murmured, and tugged at the knot on his tie. "Where's Pea?"

The mention of eight-year-old Sara Jane—Sweet Pea to her daddy—sliced sharp and cutting on Emma's heart. Sara was going to be another casualty of this little war Garrett had started. For that alone, she could never forgive him,

"I took her to Maddie's for the night."

Maddie Brannigan was Emma's best friend. Garrett understood the implication. His eyes flickered with expectant pleasure. "Overnight?"

She nodded, affecting a sultry look.

She closed her eyes as he folded her into his arms, fighting hurt, remembering love, quelling the biting sting of his betrayal.

"Drink your wine," she whispered, pulling away from his nuzzling mouth to snag his wineglass and press it to his lips.

He tasted, swallowed, smiled. "Good."

"Indulge," she prompted as he tipped the glass yet again. "You've got time for a shower before dinner if you'd like."

He set his glass on the table and touched a finger to her cheek. "I'd like. Be right back."

She watched in a numb silence as he climbed the stairs. It wasn't until she heard the bathroom door close and the sound of his shower that she slowly turned and walked on wooden legs to the kitchen.

Feeling humiliated and used, she blinked back tears, gathered her composure and let her anger work to outdistance the hurt. Taking special care, she took her time arranging a standing rib roast on a silver platter, then carried it into the dining room.

It was with a detached, leaden interest that she saw he'd finished his shower and his wine and was in the process of refilling his glass and pouring one for her.

His hair was still wet, shining almost blue-black by

candlelight. His eyes danced as he turned and saw her standing there. He extended the shimmering burgundy.

"To us," she murmured, and lifted the glass to her lips in toast.

It was an invitation he couldn't refuse. "To us," he echoed softly.

Over the rim of her glass, Emma watched him tip the wine to his lips and swallow. Without touching her own, she invited him to sit down.

Then she drew a deep breath and waited for the mix of Valium and alcohol to do its work.

It didn't take long. And by the time he felt the effect, she was too numbed by grief to be horrified by what she'd done.

"This is...won...der...ful." The words stumbled out, the chemicals undercutting his attempt at enthusiasm.

He blinked twice. Shook his head, slow and woozy.

She thought of Sara Jane, of his callous disregard for ten years of marriage and watched him through hard eyes. "Is there a problem?" she asked, her voice sounding as hollow as her heart had become.

"No...yeah...I don't...know. Feeling kind...of... light...head...ed."

Unfocused, bleary eyes searched her face with disconnected confusion before they rolled back in his sockets and his eyelids fluttered shut. His fork clattered to his plate, then in slow, suspended motion, he tipped forward, passed-out cold.

Emma watched for a long, vacuous moment before she rose wearily and walked around the table to stand beside him.

Filling her hand with his hair, she tipped his head back and studied his face.

He was so beautiful. Too beautiful. And too hard, it seemed, for a woman to resist. His jaw was strong and wide. Deep grooves ran the length of his cheeks, defining and showcasing the rugged masculinity of his mouth, the sensual curve of his lips. She ran a trembling finger down the length of his face, then threaded and rethreaded her fingers through his hair.

Finally she let the tears fall.

"You cheating bastard," she whispered into a room full of the sumptuous aroma of the meal she'd prepared and the sour scent of heartbreak. "How could you do this to me? How could you do this to *us?* You had no right. You had no right to let another woman—" she choked back a sob "—to let another woman touch our marriage."

Or your hair, she thought with an aching sadness for the innocent promises of youth as she lovingly fingered his coarse blue-black strands for the last time.

On leaden legs she climbed the stairs and walked to the master bathroom. With trembling hands she opened the medicine cabinet.

The weight of his razor felt deceptively light as she slid it from the shelf and held it in her hand.

The blade was new. Excessively sharp. She stared at it, then at her tear-streaked face in the mirror—and tried not to think about what she was going to do.

Garrett crawled into consciousness like a drunk clawing his way out of a gutter. He squeezed his eyes tight then willed them apart.

Mistake. Big mistake.

Pain speared like a rusty nail through his skull. It felt like someone had poured hot sand under his eyelids, then sealed them shut with superglue. His heads—all ten of them—pounded as if a team of snare drummers had taken up residence there. And his mouth—he swallowed with caution then grimaced—his mouth tasted like an animal had crawled inside and died.

He rocked slowly forward in the chair. Propping his elbows on the dining room table, he buried his face in his hands, trying to clear the mucky net of cobwebs.

"What the hell happened…?" His voice, sounding like a gear, long rusted and way past the need of oil, broke off as he ran a hand across his face then skated it up through his hair.

His heart dived to his stomach like a bungee jumper on a free fall when his hand reached the top of his head.

Oblivious, suddenly, to the pain and the grit in his eyes, he shot out of the chair. In a stumbling, drunken lurch, he raced to the mirror in the hall—then groaned in horror and disbelief at what he saw there.

It was gone! His *hair* was gone. All of it. Not a single, solitary strand was left. He'd been skinned as smooth as a cue ball.

With a half moan, half sob, he stared at his sorry reflection. Shock paralyzed him. Shock and wild bewilderment. He closed his eyes, shook his head and prayed that when he opened them again, his hair would be exactly where it was supposed to be.

Muttering a short, crude expletive when it wasn't, he studied his hairless head and discovered something else that sent his heart rate off the RPM dial. Not only was he bald—he was bleeding.

Wild-eyed, he looked closer then breathed a small sigh of relief. It wasn't blood, streaked across his naked scalp. In fact, it looked like…lipstick? He took a closer look. It *was* lipstick. The same color of lipstick Emma wore.

Brows furrowed in confusion and pain, he finally realized that the lines of crimson scrawled across skin as bare and pink as a baby's bottom were actually letters. He squinted to make them out, struggling to read them backward in the mirror. Giving up, he stumbled to the desk, grabbed a note pad and pen and raced back to the mirror.

Even before he'd scribbled the last decoded letter onto the paper, he knew what it spelled out. Shoulders sagging, he stared at the message in numb shock, more stunned by the words than by the loss of his hair.

I WANT A DIVORCE glared back at him with the impact of a gut punch.

He slumped wearily against the wall, ran a hand through his nonexistent hair and closed his eyes.

"I came home to dinner," he muttered, lost in this maze of a living nightmare, and tried to retrace his steps. "My wife was slowly seducing me." He ticked off event number two on his finger.

That was as far as he got. Pushing away from the wall, he braced his palms on the hall table and hung his head. He didn't remember a thing past that point. Not one damn thing.

Slowly he raised his head. In a daze, he stared at his sorry self in the mirror again, then let go of a near-hysterical snort of laughter.

"There's a bright side, here, James," he advised his reflection, while humor as black as his lost hours brought a twisted smile to his lips. "You won't be having any bad-hair days in your immediate future."

"*What* did you do to your hair?"

Garrett waited patiently on his mother-in-law's front porch for the color to bleed back into her face.

"Viola," he said calmly, working past her wide-eyed stare, "is Emma here?"

Viola DuPree studied her son-in-law's bald head. Narrowing her pale brown eyes in accusation, she crossed her arms dramatically beneath the small shelf of her breasts. "I *knew* it would happen someday. You went off the deep end, didn't you? You just got too busy working all those hours, making all that money, and you snapped. You joined one of those cults, didn't you, dear?"

For as long as he'd known her, Viola had lived in her own little world, with her own skewed take on life. She was sweet and harmless, and until today her perceptions had rarely affected him. Today, however, he needed her to be lucid. Even rational. Struggling to keep a rein on his impatience, he measured his words to encourage that result. "Please, Vi, I need to find Emma. Just tell me if she's here."

His mother-in-law eyed him with a delicacy born of her Southern breeding but with unmistakable disdain. "You cult people always want money. I know about these things. I *do* read. For shame, Garrett. Don't think that just because you're my son-in-law that you can bilk me out of my money because it's not going to happen. I tithe to my church and I don't believe in any of—"

"Viola," he interrupted sternly, before she went off so far afield of his question that he'd never get her back on track. "I did *not* join a cult. I do *not* want your money. I just want to find Emma. Do you know where she is?"

"A swim team," she suggested, after a long pause that told him there was little hope of making a connection. "Is that it? You joined a swim team? I see pictures of those boys all the time, and they always shave their heads. But thirty-three's a little old, don't you think, to get into competitive swimming? I know you're in good shape and all, but really, Garrett, you've got to be a bit more practical. It's just like that fancy black foreign car you bought last spring. Not practical—"

Garrett gripped her by her shoulders, his patience at its end. Aware of the fragility of her sparrowlike bones beneath his strong hands, he kept his hold gentle. "Viola. Please. Just listen to me. Really listen now, okay? I did *not* join a cult. I did *not* join a swim team. I did *not* shave my head. Emma did this to me. She tried to seduce me, then she must have drugged me...." He paused to collect himself. It was hard to think the words, let alone say them, but it was the only scenario he could come up with. "And then she shaved my head," he continued, as Viola's eyes took on a glazed look. "I need to find her, Viola, so I can figure out what's going on."

Viola removed herself carefully from his grip and backed a cautious step away. "I...I think I need my medication." Her eyes darted uneasily past him to the street, then back to him again.

She smiled with care. "Why don't you go sit in your car and wait for a moment," she suggested with the slow and deliberate patience of a wise and compassionate zookeeper soothing a rabid rabbit. "I'll take my medicine and then I'll just go call 911 and they can come and help you find her. You'd like that, wouldn't you? A nice ride in a big white van? It has a siren. Boys always like sirens."

He smothered an oath, forced a weary breath and collected his control. In the most calm voice he could manage, he tried one last time. "Viola. Look. I know this sounds crazy, but believe me, *I'm* not. And I'm beginning to worry that Emma might be having a...I don't know...she's seemed unhappy lately. Not herself. Maybe...maybe she's having a breakdown or something.

"Look, I know it's hard to believe, but Emma *did* do this to me. And now she's gone and I don't know where she is or where Pea is. I'm worried sick. I need to find them."

Viola stared, her eyes cautious, considering.

"I swear to God, Viola. I'm as sane as you are." He winced the moment the words were out. Pitting his mental state against his mother-in-law's was not a viable comparison. "Please, Viola. Just tell me. Have you seen her?"

Evidently enough of his concern bled through that she finally decided to believe him. "No, dear. I haven't. And I don't know where she is, either. But one thing I do know. If my Emma did this to you, she must have had one exceedingly good reason."

Leveling him with that nonnegotiable indictment, she slammed the door in his face.

"Great," he muttered as he turned and walked to his car. "Just great."

With a grind of gears and a squeal of tires, he headed for Maddie's, hoping to find his answers there.

"Let's get this straight up front. I don't need any of your lip," Garrett warned Maddie Brannigan, when Emma's best friend opened her apartment door, stared long and hard, then burst into a spasm of giggles.

At five foot two, with a muppet's mop of dusky blond curls and wearing a long paisley skirt and oversize pink, cotton sweater, Maddie looked as harmless and as displaced as a flower child from the sixties. He reminded himself that jellyfish also looked harmless and that Maddie also had a mouth that could cut like a buzz saw.

"I mean it, Maddie. I've just about reached my limit and I do not—I repeat—*do not* want to hear one word from you about my hair."

"What hair?" she asked, deadpan, fought to hold her straight face but dissolved again into a fit of snorts that she tried to cover with her hands. She failed miserably.

"Do you know where Emma is?" He enunciated each word through clenched teeth.

The giggling ceased as abruptly as it had begun. Maddie's face hardened with the forbearance of a bodyguard protecting her charge. "If I did, I wouldn't tell you."

The contempt in her voice told Garrett he'd hit pay dirt. He planted the flat of his hand on the door frame and with belligerent tolerance made his position clear.

"I want to see her."

"Yeah, well, she doesn't want to see you, chrome dome."

There was enough acid in her tone to eat the paint off a battleship.

It took everything he had to curb his temper. "Maddie...I don't have a clue what prompted her to leave me. I came home from work. I sat down to a meal. The next thing I knew, I was slumped over the table, my hair lying in piles around my feet and a message in lipstick scrawled across my head telling she wants a divorce."

"Yeah, well, she could have said it with flowers," Maddie countered with all the sweetness of alum, "but somehow, I think this way had much more impact."

"What the hell is going on!" he exploded, and shoved his foot in the door when she tried to slam it in his face. "I'm her husband, dammit! I have a right to know."

"You lost your rights when you decided to romance your blond bimbo in broad daylight, buddy." She poked a blunt-nailed finger into his chest. "If I was a man, I'd punch you out good, you low-life, philandering jackass!"

One word in the midst of her diatribe struck out and slapped him in the face. "Philandering? Wait a minute—"

"No, *you* wait a minute. You made a mistake, Mr. Big Shot Contractor. Mr. Lady-Killer. Mr. Two-Timing Double-Dealer. Mr. Fill In The Blank With Any Ugly, Derogatory Adjective You Can Think Of. You hurt my best friend. And if you think for one minute—"

"Maddie—you *know* me. I love Emma. I am *not* cheating on her."

For one fleeting, hopeful moment, she did believe him. At least she wanted to. He could see it in her eyes in the instant before they filled with venom. "I *thought* I knew you. Now all I know is that you hurt her. Dammit, Garrett. You hurt her! That makes you slime in my book. And it sure as the devil doesn't get you into my home to see her."

With that, she grabbed an umbrella from the stand by the door and jabbed it hard at his abdomen.

The sharp, sudden jolt of pain buckled his knees. He doubled over with an "oomph," clutching his arms around his middle as the door slammed in his face.

Gasping for breath, he staggered backward into the hall, his eyes squeezed shut against the involuntary sting of pain-induced tears. In a blind stumble, he hit the hallway wall with his shoulder and crumpled slowly to the floor.

"Nuts," he gritted out as he slumped there, catching his breath, riding out the pain. "Every…last…one of them…are…nuts."

When he could take a breath that didn't feel like it would rip his guts out, he eased to his feet and slunk out of the apartment building like the snake everyone thought he was.

Two

Monday morning Garrett strode stiffly into the suite of offices that housed James Construction Company, which he and Clay ran as partners. Agnes Crawford, their secretary since Jonathan James had founded the company back in the sixties, opened her mouth, then wisely shut it. She correctly read his glacial glare as a warning. Touching a nervous hand to her blue-gray hair, she watched in wary silence from behind the round frames of her trifocals as he walked directly to his private office and slammed the door behind him.

Garrett sank down in the leather chair behind his desk and waited. He knew it wouldn't be long. Agnes had no doubt reached for the phone and dialed Clay's extension as soon as Garrett had closed his door. He also knew there was nothing for it but to suffer through it.

Fortunately he just had Clay to contend with today. Only the wind knew where Jesse was. He could be anywhere from Cheyenne to Fort Worth as he worked the pro rodeo circuit, chasing his dream of a PRCA world championship in bull riding.

Garrett hadn't even reached a ten count when Clay rapped a knuckle on the door then barged in without an invitation.

"Don't start," Garrett warned with a deadly edge that anyone but his brothers would have had the good sense to heed.

Squinting as if in deep thought, Clay crossed his arms over his chest and leaned back against the closing door.

"You look different today," he observed conversationally. "I can't quite pinpoint what it is, though, with the light reflecting off your head that way." Nudging aside a black leather vest, he fished a pair of sunglasses out of the breast pocket of his shirt and slipped them on. "Hell of a glare in here."

Garrett clenched his jaw. "You're pushing it."

"*I'm* pushing it?" Clay barked, whipping off the glasses and shoving away from the door. "When Emma gets a load of your Michael Jordan hair *don't*, she's going to burst a vein. Maaannn…this is scary, Garrett."

Garrett got as far as five on a ten count. "I didn't do this."

Clay grunted. "Which means you paid someone else to. That's even scarier."

Garrett met his brother's eyes. "Emma did it."

Clay's brows lowered in disbelief before he broke into a crooked, speculative grin. "Kinky."

With a weary breath, Garrett rose and shoved his hands deep into his pants pockets. Shoulders hunched in defeat, he turned his back on his brother and walked to the window. "She left me."

He didn't have to turn around to know that Clay's jaunty stance had deflated to a troubled slouch.

"Oh," he said.

"Yeah." Absently fingering the change in his pocket, Garrett stared out the window. "Oh."

"What the hell happened?"

He shook his head. "I wish I knew. From the bits and pieces I've scraped together, it would seem she thinks I'm cheating on her."

Another contemplative "Oh" from Clay was followed by "Then I'd say you're damn lucky she didn't take that razor to something else."

Garrett turned slowly away from the window. "What am I going to do?"

Clay regarded him with a concerned frown. Garrett was always the one who was asked that question by his brothers. He was the one they always turned to. He was the one they depended on for answers. Sobered by the turn of events, Clay asked softly, "Let's back up to what *did* you do?"

"You know me better than that."

"Yeah," Clay said, watching Garrett's face carefully. "I do. Then the question is, why does Emma think you're messing around?"

Garrett sank back down in his chair. "I had a business lunch with Gloria Richards on Friday."

"Oh, boy." Those two small words encompassed a wealth of understanding. "She come on to you again, did she?"

Garrett snorted. "Like a Sherman Tank. I thought I had it covered. I made reservations at Shady's—you know that open-air restaurant down on 5th and 22nd? I figured that if we were out in public with God and the free world—and evidently Emma—watching, the woman would keep her hands to herself.'' He toyed absently with a paper clip then tossed it aside and rocked back in his chair. ''Emma must have been there and seen Gloria doing her octopus routine.''

Clay whistled long and low. ''Talk about rotten timing.''

''Yeah.'' With a lost look, Garrett scrubbed a hand across his face.

''Have you tried to talk to her?''

''That's the problem. I can't get near her. Anyway, that's part of the problem.'' He backtracked thoughtfully as Clay settled a hip on the edge of his desk. ''I know she's been unhappy lately—but I don't understand why she was so ready to believe what she thought she saw. And why didn't she just confront me so we could talk it out? Why did she—'' he raised an open palm in the general direction of his head ''—do this?''

Clay shook his head sagely. ''At the risk of repeating myself, consider yourself lucky all you lost is your hair. It's a renewable resource. Various other body parts are not.''

Clay's attempt at humor fell as flat as the stack of invoices on Garrett's desk—just as the room fell silent with the weight of Garrett's misery. Garrett buried his face in his hands.

Clay's misery grew to match. ''This is my fault.''

Garrett's head shot up. ''Your fault?''

''You work too many hours, Garrett. You take on too much of the responsibility around here. I shouldn't let that happen. I should make you go home to your family.''

''You can't make me do anything. And you more than pull your weight. Besides, I squeeze out time when I can.''

"Yeah? When? When was the last time you got home before seven? The last time you took a weekend off— and I'm not counting Sunday afternoon from three o'clock on as a weekend."

Garrett's sober frown and the guilt that weighted down his shoulders had Clay backing off.

"Hey," he said, reaching across the desk and clamping a hand on Garrett's shoulder. "Do you love her?"

The look Garrett shot him provided a definitive answer.

Clay's return look was just as conclusive. "Then fix it. Go get her back."

"Right. Between her steel magnolia of a mother and her pit bull of a best friend," he paused, his hand rising automatically to rub the tender spot on his midsection that bore the sting of Maddie's anger, "I haven't been able to get within shouting distance of her all weekend."

This time it was Clay who paced to the window. After a long moment of thought he spun around, a huge smile splitting his face. "Then there's only one recourse that I can see."

Garrett shifted in the chair, eyed him warily. "And that would be—"

An outlaw gleam shone in Clay's eyes. "I've always wanted to explore the kind of mind-set it requires to stage a kidnapping. This appears to be a golden opportunity."

With a muttered oath, Garrett buried his face in his hands. "Go away."

"Well, it was just a thought," Clay said with a sheepish shrug, then had the good sense to back out the door and shut it softly behind him.

* * *

Emma didn't jump anymore when Maddie's phone rang—but she still didn't answer it.

Watching through vacant eyes, she absently stroked Maxwell, Maddie's purring calico tomcat who was curled up on her lap. She responded to the call as she had since the night she'd moved into Maddie's apartment. She waited for the fourth ring and listened to Maddie's short, upbeat voice-mail message announce that she wasn't available. Then she tried to ignore the sound of Garrett's voice as it filled the echoing silence of the afternoon.

"Emma, please. Pick up the phone. I know you're there."

With the animation of a statue, Emma stared past the phone and out Maddie's third-floor apartment window.

A week had passed since she'd left him. A week of dealing with the guilt of what she'd done to him and refusing his calls. A week of justifying that his actions were responsible for driving her to the edge of the deep end that night.

Somehow she'd made it through the last few days of the school year. But if Garrett could see her, he'd know she was hovering on a very dangerous edge. She was a mess: she'd lost weight; she didn't eat; she didn't sleep; and since that first night, she hadn't even been able to cry.

"Emma. Don't do this to us."

The ache behind her eyes foreshadowed tears that never came, as Garrett's voice—his gruffly velvet voice that had whispered to her in the night and promised her forever—threatened to breach her resistance again.

But no matter how many times he called, no matter how much pain she heard in his words, it only took the picture of him with that woman to harden what was left of her heart.

"Em…how can we fix this if you won't talk to me?"

Every day he called. Sometimes four, five times a day. Every day she steeled herself against the wanting to believe there was something left to fix.

"Fine. Don't talk. Don't do anything but sit there and throw away what was once the most important thing in our lives. I'm tired, Emma. I can't do this much longer. I can't…"

His voice trailed off, setting her senses on alert.

"I just can't," he repeated sounding so weary, so beaten, her heart twisted for the ache in his.

"Look, just…just tell Pea I love her. Will you do that for me? And tell her I'll see her tomorrow at four in the park. And, dammit, Emma, tell Maddie or who-ever's playing bodyguard not to leave with her if I'm a few minutes late. Yesterday couldn't be helped. I got tied up in a conference call and Clay was late taking over. I've got to see her again, Emma. Without you…" His voice broke. The brief pause that followed was filled with his struggle for control. "Without you… she's all I've got left."

A deep, echoing silence passed, then the line went dead.

Emma dropped her head back against the sofa. Her throat felt so tight she couldn't swallow.

She may have left him, she may want to rip his heart out for what he'd done, but she hadn't stopped loving him. She doubted that she ever would. And she couldn't deny him his daughter. Just like she couldn't deny Sara her daddy's love. He was a good father. He always had been. Even with all the hours he worked he managed to find time for Sara. It was the part about being a husband where he'd dropped the ball.

Maddie, standing silent and supportive behind her all this time, lowered a hand to her shoulder. Emma covered it with her own before she set the disgruntled tom aside, rose from Maddie's overstuffed, abstract-print sofa and headed for the kitchen. On the way to the coffeepot, she raked her fingers through her hair, thinking as she did that it was as dull and lifeless to the touch as she felt.

Maddie followed but lingered in the doorway. "Second thoughts?" she ventured finally.

"Second? Try third. Hundreds. Thousands," Emma muttered in self-disgust and, ignoring the tremor in her hand, filled a mug with coffee. She raised it halfway to her lips, then let it hit the counter again with a soft thud. She sucked in a deep breath then exhaled wearily. "It's just…it's so damn hard."

Barefoot, her long skirt rustling, Maddie shuffled up beside her. "Men are pigs."

Maddie's indignant indictment finally made Emma smile. "What a novel summation. I don't think I've ever heard it put so eloquently before. Especially from a woman who has a date an average of two-point-five nights a week."

"Yeah, well." Maddie shot for a throwaway grin as she hiked herself up and settled her bottom onto the counter. "They have their purposes. The problem is getting rid of them when they've been served."

The blatantly hedonistic statement brought another slow, tired smile. "You are not a user, Matilda, no matter how well you bluff."

"Well, I'm certainly not marriage material," Maddie muttered with a sniff as she stretched back and riffled through the cookie jar. "But I've had a hell of a lot of fun pretending to audition for the part."

Though her heart wasn't in it, Emma grinned at her friend's innuendo à la Mae West. "You're not a tramp, either."

"And you're a real spoilsport," Maddie sputtered around a mouthful of chocolate-chip cookie, her relief at Emma's slight lift of mood evident. "You're systematically ruining my bad reputation." She offered Emma half of the cookie.

Emma shook her head. "That's because I'm into ruining things these days. Reputations. Moods. Marriages. Specifically my own."

Maddie's grin faded. She shook what was left of her cookie at her. "Hold it right there. I will not allow you to take this on your shoulders. *You're* not the one who was playing around."

Emma stared at her hands. "But I'm the one who drove him to it."

Maddie swore softly but roundly before trying again. "Emma—"

"I didn't say what he did was justified. And I didn't say I forgive him for it. I'm just admitting that I had a part to play in this, too."

"What part? What could you have possibly done?"

Emma turned away. She'd done plenty. Two years ago, when she should have turned toward him, she'd turned away. But she'd hurt so much when she'd lost the baby. Their baby that they'd tried for years to conceive. Their baby, only weeks old in her womb but loved so deeply in their hearts.

How she'd failed him then wasn't something she'd come to terms with. Just like she still hadn't come to terms with the loss of that precious life that had grown inside her.

"It took both of us to get to this point. I just—I just didn't realize—I didn't think I'd pushed him this far. I didn't think anything would ever push him this far."

When the panic hit, she should have been ready for it. But as it always did, it struck hard and swift and without warning.

She clutched the coffee mug with both hands to quell the violent trembling that gripped her. Her eyes were wild when she turned to Maddie. "My God, what have I done? I drugged him. How could I have done that?"

"He deserved worse. And you were hurt," Maddie defended gently. "And scared."

"Nobody deserves what I did to him. And I wasn't just hurt. I was out of control." She dragged her hair from her face with both hands, feeling like she was drowning in a sea of self-doubt. "I still am. Sometimes...sometimes I don't think I even know who I am anymore."

"Well, I know who you are. And what you are. And I know what you aren't." Maddie scooted off the counter and touched a supporting hand to Emma's shoulder. "You are not crazy. And you are not immune to pain. All you did was react to it. And dammit, you were entitled.

"You were entitled," she repeated with feeling when Emma's eyes swam with unshed tears of guilt and humiliation. "If I'd been holding the razor, he'd be singing soprano about now."

When her attempt at teasing her out of a smile failed, Maddie tried again. "Okay. So your reaction was extreme. A little dangerous even. That doesn't mean you aren't entitled to a little latitude. Even you, steady, sensible, enduring Emma James has a breaking point. That doesn't change who you are.''

"And who am I? Can you tell me that?'' Desperation clawed and twisted inside her.

"You're the woman who opted for natural childbirth when everyone around you was rooting for an epidural,'' Maddie reminded her forcefully. "You're the woman who took on the school board over the book ban and won. You're a wonderful mother and a good person. You're strong and you're resilient. And you're going to come out of this and show Garrett James and everybody else in this town what you're made of.''

Well-intended words. Emma wished she could believe them—like she'd believed in Garrett. Like she'd believed in the strength of their marriage.

"Give yourself some time.'' Maddie's soft reassurance infiltrated her thoughts. "You're stronger than you think. You'll sort it out. You'll get through this.''

Yeah, Emma thought with a dispassionate sigh. She'd get through this. But at what cost?

Garrett couldn't believe what he was seeing. He'd been waiting in the park since three-thirty, making damn sure Viola or Maddie didn't find an excuse to leave with Sara before he got to see her.

But it wasn't either one of them who drove up to the south side of the park, got out of the car and walked Sara toward him.

It was Emma.

His heart slammed into a wild rumble. Slowly he rose from the merry-go-round, dusted playground sand off the seat of his jeans and walked hesitantly to meet them.

When Sara saw him, she broke into a huge grin. Running at a coltish lope, she launched herself into his arms.

"Daddy!" she cried as he scooped her up and hugged her against his chest.

Giggling and squeezing for all she was worth, she wrapped her arms around his neck, her legs around his waist and clung for dear life.

"Hey, baby." He buried his face in the downy softness of her neck, smelling sunshine and life and a hint of her mother's favorite perfume. He treasured it all, the silk of her hair, the baby softness of her cheek, the look in Emma's eyes as she watched them from a distance.

"How's the sweetest pea in the garden?" he finally managed as he squatted on his haunches and set Sara back so he could look at her.

It was all he could do to pinch back tears as Sara scolded him for calling her by that baby name, then looked at him with her mother's soulful brown eyes. "I miss you, Daddy."

"Me, too, baby," he murmured, fighting the husky break in his voice. "Me, too. But we'll make up for it today, okay?"

"Okay!" she agreed with the innocent trust of youth that shattered what was left of the pieces of his heart.

With a shy smile and an expectant look, she asked the inevitable question. "Can I touch it?"

He couldn't stop a chuckle. "All right." Feigning impatience, he tugged off his black Stetson and let her rub his head.

She squealed in delight. "It tickles."

"That's because it's growing back."

"I'm glad," she whispered confidentially. "I like you better with hair. Jamie's grampa doesn't have any hair either, but she says his won't grow back 'cause he's bald."

"Well, I'm a ways from worrying about that possibility. It'll all grow back in a couple of months. Does that work for you?"

She nodded.

"Now, have you had your fill?"

After one last nuggie that sent her into another giggle fest, he resettled his hat.

"Would you care if I talk to your mom for a minute before we get on with our afternoon?"

Sara's pixie face pinched with worry as she looked from her father to her mother. "Okay. Can I go see Cary while you guys talk? She's over at the jungle gym."

Garrett glanced over his shoulder in the direction Sara pointed. Confirming that Sara's friend was there, he looked back to Emma. "Okay with you, Em?"

When she hesitated, then gave in with a quick nod, he gave Sara Jane one last hug. With a soft pat on her bottom, he sent her on her way to play with her friend.

And then for the longest time, he just stood there, one palm cupping the back of his neck, the other stuffed in his hip pocket, both sweating like those of a prisoner who was walking death row.

He'd waited for this moment. He'd rehearsed what he was going to say if he ever got the chance. Now it was here…and all he could do was look at her. At the hollowness of her cheeks, at the lack of life in her wide-set eyes, at the aloofness that cloaked her like a shield. In spite of it all, she was still the most beautiful woman he'd ever seen.

She'd always been his brown-eyed girl. He'd seen those coffee-colored eyes mist over with tears of joy, smile without pretense or care, darken for him with the heat of passion. Even the distrustful way she watched him now couldn't dull the memories or lessen the impact of seeing her again.

She'd let her long hair flow free. Filtered sunlight caught its chestnut sheen, sparking highlights of red and gold. An uncommonly crisp June breeze lifted it from her shoulders, whipped a flyaway strand across her face. It was a face that haunted him at night, shadowed him during the day.

Those round, wide-set eyes were framed by features both delicate and intriguingly bold. Her mouth was full, her cheekbones classically high. Everything about her was classic. Everything about her made him think of southern nights and supple woman—even the pale, elegant hand she raised to brush her windswept hair back behind her ear.

It was then he saw she'd taken off her wedding ring.

Something inside him shattered. Something inside him died. He should have expected it. But he hadn't been prepared. He hadn't been prepared for any of this.

"Sara…she looks good," he finally offered in an attempt to break the tension and pull himself back together.

Emma nodded, her hands shoved deep in the pockets of her light, unconstructed white linen jacket, her gaze resolutely and deliberately fixed on the ground at his feet. "She misses you."

"And that's my fault?" The accusation and the harshness at which he leveled it came out before he could stop it—and relayed all the frustration and misery he felt over losing not only his wife but his daughter.

Her eyes cut to his and for the first time, he saw a flicker of life. "Yes," she said evenly. "I believe you could say it is."

He covered his jaw with his palm, looked away, drew

a deep breath, then fixed his gaze on her again. "I didn't cheat on you, Em. I know what you thought you saw—"

"Please, don't."

Her voice was so void of emotion, her eyes so empty of tears, it frightened him.

His carefully planned reason collapsed under the weight of that fear. "Don't what? Don't defend myself? Don't wish to hell that you would talk to me and tell me why you think I'd even look at another woman, let alone take one to bed?"

She shook her head, slowly backed away. "I can't do this, Garrett. I can't. I just want to get on with my life."

"*Your* life?" he countered, working against the pain and the anger to keep his voice low. "What happened to *our* life?"

"Our life," she echoed with a hopelessness that almost brought him to his knees. "Our life—together— is over. It has been for a while now. It...it was just a question of me opening my eyes and seeing it."

The finality in her tone stunned him into silence. The emptiness in her eyes humbled him into submission.

"What do you want from me, Em? What can I say to you that will make you believe me? For godsake, what did I do? What did I do to lose your trust?"

For a moment he saw her weaken and want and hurt the way he was hurting—then he hated himself for the small twist of triumph he felt knowing he wasn't alone in his pain. But her indifference sped back in a heartbeat. She wrapped it around her like a wall of concrete and barbwire.

"I won't keep you from seeing Sara," she said in an evenly modulated tone and purposefully ignored his questions. "That's why I brought her today instead of sending her with Maddie or Mother. To tell you that myself, and to ask you not to call me anymore."

He balled his hands into fists to keep from reaching for her and shaking her until he broke her. But she was already broken. And so fragile he was afraid that if he touched her, if he said the wrong thing, it would be the end of them both.

"I need to get on with my life, Garrett. I can't do it with you constantly reminding me of my failures."

The breath slammed out of him. "Your failures? Emma. What the hell are you talking about?"

She shivered, but didn't flinch. "I'm trying to tell you that I accept my share of the blame. I can do that much. But what I can't do, is be your wife anymore."

Her words blurred, tangled, bled him of the power of reason, sucked him of the will to fight. "I don't understand. Not any of this."

"Then I guess that's something you'll have to figure out on your own."

He swallowed hard. "Whatever happened to figuring things out together?"

"Life happened," she said with such bitterness and certainty he wasn't sure if he knew her anymore. "Yours and mine. And somewhere along the line it ended up not being ours."

She waited the space of several slow, heavy breaths. "If you won't file, I will."

The earth rocked beneath his feet. Somehow, he found the presence of mind to speak. "I don't want a divorce." He enunciated each word with calculated control—a control he was far from feeling. "I want you. I want us. I want my family back."

The last words erupted on a shout of frustration so

heated, it attracted the concerned stares of an elderly couple strolling by several yards away.

"I want you back," he repeated on a ragged whisper as he strode deliberately toward her.

She met his gaze one last time. And one last time she refused to respond to his plea. "Maddie will be waiting for Sara outside the apartment at eight."

Her calm control sapped the last of his. "To hell with Maddie. To hell with seeing you by accident and Sara according to some goddamn timetable. You're my wife. She's my child."

She blinked once, slowly, then turned and headed for the car.

"How can you just walk away from this?" He didn't think, didn't weigh the consequences as he grabbed her arm and spun her around to face him. "Tell me...tell me you don't love me anymore and I'll leave you alone."

His words boiled out, demanding an answer he knew he might not want to hear. But he was past reason, beyond caution. "Tell me you don't miss this, and I'll never bother you again."

Pinning her with his gaze, he hauled her hard against him, then crushed her in his arms where she belonged.

Instinct took over then. Instinct and need.

He covered her mouth with his, sank into her softness, savored her familiar, sultry scent. God, he'd missed the taste of her, the feel of her beneath his hands, molded to his body.

With a groan that came from low in his throat, he deepened the contact, fed on the flavor he'd been addicted to since he'd stolen his first kiss. With each thrust of his tongue he told her it had been too long. He needed too much. He wanted too badly.

On some level he knew that possession and greed played as big a part in his actions as love did. That knowledge didn't ease the rough glide of his hands over her back. Couldn't stop the intimate press of his hips that demanded she give him back the response he needed.

What he couldn't accomplish with words, what he couldn't coerce with his kiss, he prayed that a greater power could. All the while he held her, he prayed to God that the woman in his arms would come back to life as the woman he had loved.

But his prayers weren't answered.

And her response never came.

With an ache so huge it left him shaking, he slowly pulled away. The eyes that had once warmed his were as cold as winter. The expressive face he'd loved forever was as empty of emotion as a block of wood.

"Tell me you don't love me," he repeated, an urgent demand, a rusty plea for a response he wasn't sure he could handle, didn't want to hear.

All he heard was her silence.

And all he would see for days and nights to come was the sight of her walking away.

Three

"I love you, sweetheart, but quite frankly, you look like hell." Maya James Bradford delivered her frank assessment of her son's appearance with characteristic candor.

Though he gave up a weary smile, Garrett didn't look up from the set of blueprints spread across his drafting table. "I see marriage hasn't done anything to take the edge off your tongue, Mother."

It had been three months since Maya and Logan Bradford had exchanged vows. Close to three weeks since Emma had left him. Not a day had passed that he hadn't missed her or agonized over how he could get her back. While he wasn't up to expressing it, he was pleased to see his mother so obviously happy. He was not pleased to see her in his office tonight—especially since the first words out of her mouth foreshadowed where her visit was leading.

"This isn't like you, Garrett." She eased onto a stool beside him.

He glanced at her then, saw the color love had painted in her cheeks, took stock of the fact that in her late fifties, she was still an attractive, vital woman. Silently, he congratulated Logan Bradford on his good taste and good fortune, and tried to steer the conversation away from himself to her.

"And that particular suit isn't like you, either," he said, forcing a teasing tone that not only got the smile he wanted but hopefully distracted her from the little heart-to-heart she had in mind. "Showing a lot of leg these days. Not that they aren't great legs," he added when she narrowed her eyes.

"I think it falls into the category of new leaves—"

"And new love?" he offered, truly happy for her. "Speaking of which, how is Logan?"

"Logan is wonderful," she stated without preamble or hesitation. "But it's not Logan I came here to talk about."

"If you came here to talk about Emma and me, just don't start, okay?"

He let out a deep breath, disgusted with himself over the bite he'd just taken out of his mother.

"I'm sorry. I didn't mean to snipe at you."

"And I didn't mean to open any wounds. It's just that I don't understand why you two are still apart. You love each other. You always have."

"In the immortal words of Tina Turner, 'What's love got to do with it?'"

He wasn't proud of his sarcasm. Grim-faced, he stared at the blueprints without really seeing them. "She wants it over. She's made it clear. And I'm done begging. I can only swallow so much pride."

When he fell silent, she rested a gentle hand on his arm. "I don't mean to interfere—but I want you to think about something. Your father—you're so like him," she reflected softly before continuing. "Your father never would have given up on something he believed in."

He closed his eyes and swallowed hard.

"If you believe in your love, then your pride is the only thing getting in your way. Take some time away from the business—you're long overdue, anyway—and go after her.

"But for now, for heaven's sake, go home," she added after touching her hand to his hair. "It's late. And you work too hard."

After a long look at his silent profile, she gave up and left him.

Since that day in the park, Garrett had honored Emma's wishes and left her alone. His mother was right, though. Pride had as much to do with that decision as Emma's request. Even in late June, however, pride was a hell of a cold companion at night. But despite what his mother had said, pride was also the only thing that kept him going. That and his visits with Sara.

His work made the days pass. Nothing helped with the nights. Oh, Gloria was always waiting in the wings. Her invitation was consistent and clear. He didn't even consider taking her up on it. He didn't want another woman in his bed. He wanted Emma. And he began to hate himself for that weakness, even as he prayed that if he gave her some time, she'd change her mind.

Though he had yet to sign them, the day that Emma had served him with divorce papers, he'd finally accepted that she really wanted it over between them. Sara, in her innocence, however, just wouldn't let it rest.

"Mommy has a summer job at Aunt Maddie's," she announced one day over a burger and fries at her favorite fast-food restaurant.

Maddie's shop was an upscale, artsy gallery that catered to the "resettlement crowd" of celebrities and multimillionaires who claimed the Jackson Hole area with its spectacular view of the Tetons and its wealth of equally spectacular and pricey building sites as their second homes. Her shop, Necessities, showcased and sold not only Maddie's original works of pottery, but exhibited sculptures, weavings and multiple medias of art on canvas of other local artisans.

"She's a girl Friday," Sara said proudly, referring to her mother, then wrinkled her little nose and asked with open confusion, "What's a girl Friday?"

At the first mention of Emma's name, Garrett had lost the taste for his french fries. He leaned back, shoved them aside. "Oh, it's kind of like a helper. She probably watches the shop for Maddie, takes care of customers, that sort of thing."

Sara considered, then nodded. "Prob'ly."

"Does she like it?" He couldn't help himself from asking any more than he could stop his next thought from forming. Emma had always enjoyed her summers off. Had enjoyed the extra time at home. She used to enjoy a lot of things, he thought glumly—like being his wife.

Sara shrugged, oblivious to the self-examination of his failings. "Maddie pays her money. I think she likes that. She says maybe we'll be moving out on our own soon."

He slumped back in the molded plastic booth and looked absently out the window. "Will that make her happy, do you think? Being out on her own?"

Sara twisted her elfin mouth into a frown and gave him a huge shrug. "I sure hope so. Mommy's never happy anymore."

Mommy's never happy anymore.

Sara's innocently revealing words should have given Garrett a measure of satisfaction as they echoed through his mind in the days to come. He tried to tell himself he was glad Emma was hurting—the way he'd been hurting since she'd walked out his door and taken his life with her.

But the thought of her misery only increased his own. He couldn't bear to think of her in pain—had been so busy nursing his own wounds, he'd deliberately discounted the weight of hers.

Mommy's never happy anymore.

He'd thought he had too much pride. But in the end pride didn't factor into the equation.

The summer night was warm when he walked down the street and stopped outside Necessities. With an ache in his gut, Garrett watched through half an inch of plate glass as Emma moved about Maddie's shop. She looked so beautiful, yet so wooden and removed it scared the hell out of him. It had been less than a month since she'd left him, but already she was a shadow of the warm, giving woman who was his wife. A ghost of the girl who had smiled with her eyes and loved with all her heart.

Your father never would have given up on something he believed in. Just like Sara's words, his mother's words had played like a recording day after day in his mind—but it only took seeing his wife again to finally send the message home. He *had* given up. He'd given up on her. Worse, he'd given up on them.

What a pathetic, sorry excuse for a man. He'd been so mired in self-pity, so embedded in the righteousness of being wronged, he'd given up. Bottom line, he'd quit.

Garrett James had never been a quitter. Never walked away from a fight. Yet he'd turned his back on the most important battle of his life.

Not anymore. Right then, right there, he decided that despite the divorce papers that were still shoved, unsigned in a desk drawer, he was going to fight the fight. And he had no intention of fighting fair.

"Hot damn," Clay exploded with a whoop of excited laughter as he and Jesse met with Garrett several weeks later. "We're actually going to do it."

It was close to midnight as they sat around the table in Garrett's kitchen and finalized the plan.

"Somehow, the thought of committing a federal offense shouldn't strike me as something to laugh about." This from a grinning Jesse, who shoved away from the table and reached into the fridge for another bottle of beer. "But I've got to admit, it promises to be one helluva ride."

Garrett addressed both brothers stoically. "I told you from the beginning, if you want out, tell me now and there's no harm done."

As he surveyed their faces, however, he knew they were in for the duration. They had been boys when they'd made their pact to come to each other's aid, no questions asked. But it was as men that they'd known they would be called on to keep it—just as Garrett had known when he'd placed the calls that his brothers would come. Clay was right here in Jackson, but Jesse, whom he'd caught up with in Boisie, had pulled out of an important competition to help.

The time was finally here, Garrett thought with equal measures of determination and relief. Once he'd made up his mind, it had taken him the better part of a month to set his plan in motion. Too much time had passed already—he couldn't stand to wait one more minute.

"Let's do it." Garrett snagged his black Stetson and settled it firm. Clay and Jesse, also dressed in black, rose with a scrape of chair legs on the tile floor and followed him out the back door.

The night was dark. The thin sliver of moon managed few appearances behind the slow-moving cover of heavy, mud gray clouds. When the black pickup pulling a horse trailer eased to a stop in the alley behind Maddie Brannigan's apartment building, it blended like the shadows into the night.

Jesse cut the headlights but left the engine softly purring and ready to make tracks. Slipping out from behind the wheel, he hung close to the trailer where he could keep the horses quiet.

Satisfied that Jesse knew his assignment, Garrett, with Clay at his side, rounded the five-story building and punched in the security code Garrett had found tucked inside Sara's shoe.

"So far so good," Clay whispered covertly as they sneaked into the building. With a furtive glance over their shoulders, they ascended the three flights of stairs to Maddie's floor.

"Now don't get carried away with theatrics," Garrett growled as they neared her door. "Just stick to the plan, and we'll get out of here before anyone knows what happened. And whatever you do," he added, all too aware of Maddie's hot temper, "don't tick her off."

Clay gave him a thumbs-up, drew in a fortifying

breath and punched the doorbell. Garrett, standing around the corner and out of the line of vision of whoever opened the door, hugged the wall and waited.

He heard the muted click of a latch, then the clunk of a security chain catch hold. Maddie's voice, muffled and sounding fuzzy from sleep, hissed into the silence. "What the devil are you doing here?"

"Hey, Maddie. Did I wake you? Sorry, but I've come up with an idea for your shop—trust me—it won't keep until morning." Clay played the apologetic but excited businessman with convincing skill.

Garrett held his breath, waiting to see if Maddie would go for the bait. Necessities had outgrown its present location months ago. With reluctance Maddie had approached the James Construction Company about building a new gallery.

Maddie had been reluctant because, in addition to her recent disapproval of Garrett, she and Clay, who'd grown up together, had never let go of a case of adolescent competitiveness. Clay used to beat her at everything from baseball to pool. He'd been a merciless, gloating victor. She'd been a vindictive loser. And she wasn't the kind to forgive and forget.

In spite of their volatile past, Maddie had a head for business and hadn't let her childhood vendetta stand in the way of what was best for her business. The James Construction Company was the best value in town. Their product was better than good and their prices competitive.

She'd been at Clay, the more intuitive of the two brothers when it came to envisioning her ideas, for weeks to come up with blueprints for her to study.

Garrett was counting on the blueprints and Maddie's

hunger to get her hands on them as his ticket into the apartment.

When she grumbled but told Clay to hold on a minute while she threw on a robe, Garrett let out a deep breath and waited for Clay to walk inside.

There was no going back now. He was either on the road to getting his life back or tomorrow he'd be facing kidnapping charges.

Garrett waited an agonizing five minutes, then moved silently to Maddie's apartment door. If Clay had done his part, it would be unlocked and Maddie would be diverted to the kitchen.

His palm was damp when he gave the knob a slow twist. When it opened without a hitch, he let out a pent-up breath and ducked inside.

Except for the light coming from the kitchen, where Clay was playing decoy and keeping Maddie occupied with the blueprints, the apartment was darkness and shadows. He shut the door silently behind him, and without drawing Maddie's attention, sidestepped the cat that sidled lazily across his path and headed down the hall.

He'd been to Maddie's many times with Emma in the past. Knew the layout well enough to bypass the door that led to Maddie's bedroom for the next one. With the stealth of a thief, he opened it and slipped inside.

His little sweet pea slept with the peace of an angel. Moving across the carpeted floor, he eased a hip on the bed and bent down to press a kiss on her brow.

She woke up with a sleepy yawn, knuckled the sleep from her eyes and smiled up at him.

"Hi, Daddy." Scrambling to her knees, she snuggled into his arms.

"Hey, sweetheart." Her hair was silk beneath his hand, her tidy little body warm and at home against his chest. "Did I interrupt any pretty dreams?"

She shook her head and scooted back so she could see his face in the faint glow of her teddy bear nightlight. "Is tonight the night?"

He tucked a ribbon of hair behind her ear. "Tonight's the night."

When he'd started making plans, he'd questioned the wisdom of confiding in her. It was a lot to lay on an eight-year-old. It was a huge secret to keep. He'd questioned even more, however, how he could live with himself if her mother's sudden absence and the accusations that were sure to follow would do more damage than the truth.

In the end he'd told her, just this afternoon, prepared to scrap the whole thing if it in any way alarmed her. He hadn't had to worry. Sara Jane had embraced the idea of him sweeping her mother away to a secret hideaway with the enthusiasm of listening to a fairy tale.

"Just like Prince Charming." Wrapping her arms around his neck, she burrowed close again. "Mommy's going to love it. And when you come back, she'll be smiling again, right?"

"Right, baby." He hugged her tight and prayed he didn't let her down. "When she comes back, she'll be smiling again."

Laying her gently back against her pillow, he pulled the coverlet up to her chin. "You go back to sleep now, okay? And dream your sweet dreams. In the morning, when your aunt Maddie is fussing and fuming like an old hen with wet feathers—" he paused and shared her smile "—you remember that your mother is safe with me and that I would never hurt her. You okay with that?''

She grinned up at him and, mimicking the gesture she'd seen her uncle Clay do hundreds of times, she gave him a double-thumbs-up sign.

"I love you, pea.''

"Love you, too, Daddy," she whispered, then nodded, a delighted co-conspirator, when he pressed a finger to his lips to signal the need for her silence.

Emma didn't sleep much anymore. And when she did, she dreamed. Restless, sultry dreams. Of Garrett. Of the two of them. Together. In love. In bed.

She'd wake up shaken. Shivering. Full of wanting. Empty of him. Always, so empty of him. She hated herself for still wanting him, still loving him after what he'd done.

Tonight was supposed to be different. Tonight she was supposed to sleep. Restful, healing sleep. Maddie promised.

Because exhaustion had taken its toll, the original teetotaler, Emma James, had let Maddie convince her that a little wine to relax her wouldn't hurt. She was not a drinker. As a teenager when her friends had experimented with alcohol, she'd abstained. Even now, the occasional half a glass of wine with dinner was the extent of her indulgence. Tonight, Maddie convinced her to break the pattern to celebrate Emma's first full month on the job at Necessities. In truth, Emma had wanted peace, a respite from the constant, suffocating heartbreak of her failed marriage.

So, she'd given in, and with a little too much help from the brothers Gallo, she'd set out to accomplish just that. She'd drunk until she'd dropped so she could sleep. Just sleep.

Maddie had helped her to bed hours ago. But here she lay. Eyes closed against the darkness. Head spinning in wild free flight. Heart pounding a heavy, sluggish warning that tonight she was slipping over the edge of yet one more place she didn't want to go.... It seemed she was dreaming again—only this time, she was wide-awake.

Every element of the night seemed magnified. The sound of her bedroom door opening and closing. The scent—Garrett's scent—of musk and male and memories of midnights in his arms. The drift of his breath on her brow.

Had the wine not had such a hold on her, she might have been wary of the vividness of her sense of Garrett's presence. Instead she savored it. Rode with it. She couldn't let herself want him in the light, but couldn't fight that wanting in the darkness. So she embraced it for the fantasy that it was.

"Emma..."

His voice whispered into the night. And when his lips brushed hers—so soft, so tender—she surrendered to whatever madness, whatever magic had conjured sensations as evocative as these. With a sigh of welcome, she opened her mouth. With a soft moan of pleasure, she invited him in.

The sweetness was essential. The warmth a haven she welcomed. She remembered this. Remembered too well the sinking, languid sensation of being surrounded by the scent of him, the heat of him, the heart of him.

How often had she felt his bold heart beat like thunder against her breast? How often had his breath mingled and mated with hers in the darkness? Woman to man. One woman to one man—the only man she'd ever loved.

With an earthy groan, he pulled away. She whimpered, stunned by the loss. Missing him again, missing him still.

"Come with me...." His whispered plea swept through her senses like a silken breeze.

But even in her dreamy, wine-fogged state, she knew she couldn't go with him. Not now. Not after she'd made it this long. She shook her head to tell him no. Yet when she touched his face, she said, "Don't go."

And in that moment of tactile awareness, with the stubble of his beard abrasive and rough against her palm, the warmth of his flesh vital and real against her fingertips, she knew. This was no dream she was spinning. This was real. This was now, and she was caught somewhere between the wanting to believe it and a frantic need to deny that it could be so.

Her eyes fluttered open. "Garr—"

The light touch of his fingertips to her lips silenced her.

"Come with me, Em...." His words were dream soft, his breath a caress in a room lit only by the faint glow of a streetlight filtering in the window. "I want this to be your choice...but, sweetheart, I don't have time to convince you."

It all snapped together then. Garrett was really here. In Maddie's apartment. In her bedroom.

"Wha—"

A gentle but firm hand covered her mouth as he pressed his cheek to hers and shushed her.

With the speed of a lightning strike, outrage set in. He had no right. He had no right to invade her dreams, steal into her bedroom and stir up fires she'd worked so hard to douse. To resurrect needs she'd buried with her hope.

She clamped her fingers around his wrist and fought to break free. Her lack of effectiveness against his strength and his patient "Shush, you'll wake up Sara" infuriated her even more.

She bucked, surprising him. Temporarily free, she scrambled across the bed—only to have his big hand snag her ankle, drag her back and effortlessly pin her beneath him.

"Em...please, just listen for a minute."

She didn't dare listen. Or feel—because everything she felt was steeped in him. His long, hard length nestled like hot steel over her body. His warm breath caressed like a promise against her jaw. His scent and the memories of making love in the dark aroused and enticed, blurring reason, shattering resolve—a resolve she'd worked so long to strengthen.

She wasn't sure where her fight came from. She wasn't even sure what she was fighting—him or her own weakness. It was her weakness that had dreamed him here; it was her weakness that had wanted him here. But it was instinct that needed him gone. She'd fought too hard, hurt too badly in her struggle to will him out of her life. She couldn't give up all the ground she'd gained in one weak, sweet moment of surrender.

The panic of uncertainty, the wild pump of adrenaline and the intoxicating rush of a full-bodied wine combined with inevitable results. She clawed like a wildcat. She fought like a tiger. She actually managed to tear herself away and rise in triumph to her feet on the other side of the bed.

Her victory, however, was short-lived and shaky. The blood left her head about the same time that the alcohol hit it. She swayed once, felt the cloak of unconsciousness surround her, then folded like a losing hand in a high-stakes poker game.

Winded and worried that Maddie would hear their scuffle, Garrett had let Emma go when she'd rolled to her feet and out of his reach. He stood slowly, ready to reason, ready, even, to plead, to apologize—anything to calm her—when he realized something was wrong.

"Em?" he whispered, then in a rare panic, vaulted across the bed and caught her just as her knees gave out.

"What the hell have you done to her?"

Maddie and Clay raised their heads in unison from the blueprints spread across her kitchen table.

"Answer me, Maddie," Garrett growled as he cradled an unconscious Emma in his arms. "What's wrong with her?"

Stunned into momentary silence, Maddie's puzzled gaze darted from one brother to the other. It didn't take long for her to put it all together. When she did, the fire in her eyes relayed even better than her words that she knew she'd been set up.

"You snakes!" She shot to her feet. "You miserable, scum—"

"Save it," he snapped, anxious and worried. "I want to know what's wrong with her."

Maddie crossed her arms belligerently beneath her breasts. "Nothing that getting you out of her head wouldn't fix."

When it was apparent they were at a stalemate, Garrett turned toward the door. "I'm taking her to the hospital."

A snort from Maddie stopped him. "Put a leash on

the heroics. She's fine—if you don't count the hangover she's going to have in the morning.''

Tension strung like a power line between his shoulders as Garrett looked down in disbelief at the limp, lifeless woman in his arms. He'd been so frightened for her. He'd thought—hell, he didn't know what he'd thought, but it sure as the world wasn't what Maddie had just implied.

He turned slowly, pinning Maddie where she stood with one hard look. "She's...drunk?"

"As a sailor on shore leave." Maddie had the decency to look a little guilty. She shrugged, uncomfortable under his condemning glare. "Well-l-l-l...it seemed like a good idea at the time. I'd forgotten she was such a lightweight."

"You got her drunk?" he ground out, disbelief wrapped around every word.

"No. *You* got her drunk, lover man," Maddie flung back, rounding the kitchen island and stalking toward the phone. "Now put her down, or so help me, I'll call the police."

"You're not calling anyone." Forcing a calming breath, he willed reason to outdistance his anger. "Look. I know you love her, too, Maddie. Because of that I'm working real hard on putting up with your lip. But whether you like it or not, I'm taking her with me."

With a steely glare that reinforced his intentions, and a meaningful nod at Clay, he headed for the door. "Keep her quiet," he ordered over his shoulder and left with his wife in his arms.

"You heard the man." An ornery grin tugged one corner of Clay's mouth. He reached for the phone cord and yanked it from the jack. "I'm supposed to keep you quiet. Now what do you suppose would be the best way to go about doing that?''

Maddie eyed him like he was an oily stain in the middle of her white carpet. ''Touch me and you'll never use those hands again,'' she warned, brandishing the phone receiver like a war club.

His grin widened. ''Then who would build your new studio? Come on, Matilda—lighten up,'' he added, playing on her common sense, even as he baited her by calling her by the name only Emma got away with using. ''You know you're just ticked off because we got the best of you. And you know Garrett would never hurt Emma. He just wants to talk to her. You can give him that, can't you? You can give her that if you're really her friend. Or does that viper mouth of yours have a stone-cold heart to go with it?''

The brief flicker of compassion in her eyes said she was weakening. Yet when her gaze darted from him to the door he knew the battle was far from over.

''You're slime, Clayton James.''

''Sweet talk'll get you nowhere, darlin'.'' His patronizing tone didn't score him any points. The starch in her back told him this was personal now.

''Really?'' Suddenly all saccharine smiles and narrowed eyes, she tossed the phone aside and closed the distance between them. ''Then maybe I'd better talk a different language—one even you will understand.''

With a sultry drop of her lashes, she touched a hand to his chest—then brought her knee up hard in his groin.

With a gasping groan, he doubled over, but managed to snag a handful of her hair just before she lunged out of reach.

They fell to the floor in a tangle of flailing limbs, shifting satin and a string of muffled curses.

"Just like...old times..." he gritted out between clenched teeth as they wrestled.

With a final roll that landed her on her back beneath him, he pinned her small frame to the floor with the weight of his body and rode out the worst of the pain.

She swore, breathless and bucking beneath him. "You can't keep me here."

Now that the pain was lessening, he was beginning to enjoy their little scuffle. "Watch me."

With a last second dodge of his head, he narrowly avoided the rake of her nails across his cheek. Pinning her hands above her head, he lowered his mouth close to hers.

"You come anywhere near my mouth with your tongue, and so help me, I'll bite it off."

She was a fireball and a shrew, and damned if she wasn't turning him on. He was debating the wisdom of putting her threat to the test when a tickle of awareness shimmied up his spine.

Maddie tuned in to the presence of their audience the same time he did.

They turned their heads in unison, both knowing it wasn't the cat who had joined them. Sara Jane stood, sleepy-eyed, in the hallway.

"Are you guys playing kissy-face?" She scowled down at them, twisting a long ribbon of hair around her finger.

"Don't...don't you think you should go back to bed, sweetheart?" Maddie suggested, her voice tight and high.

Sara shook her head with the sageness of an ancient. "That's what Daddy used to say when he and Mommy were playing kissy-face." Her big sigh was wrought with resignation as she turned and padded on her little pink bare feet back to bed.

"So," Clay said after a lengthy silence in which both of them were far too aware of the fit of their bodies and the heat of the moment. "You wanna play kissy-face?"

Maddie sucked in a deep breath and with concentrated effort leveled a chilling glare. "When cowboys ride cows."

Four

The clouds had broken by the time the club cab, with Jesse at the wheel and Garrett, with Emma curled up on his lap, reached the Wind River Range and the end of the road.

Garrett preferred to think that Emma had slept through the shift from pickup to horseback with little more than sleepy murmurs and restless sighs. In truth, he knew she was passed out cold.

"You sure she just tied one on?" Jesse glanced over his shoulder, his silhouette one with his horse as they climbed the rugged trail up the side of the mountain. "She's been out a long time."

Garrett looked down at the unconscious woman in his arms. Moonlight peeked through the ceiling of towering pine boughs, danced across the dewy soft planes of her face. He'd wrapped a sleeping bag around her to stall a chill from the coolness of the night. Gathering it a little closer to her face, he resettled her on his lap.

"She's fine," he said and willed it to be true. Her breathing was even, her sleep peaceful. There was no reason to read it as anything but a combination of exhaustion and wine.

Jesse nodded, tugged his bandanna back up over his lower face to protect it from the slap of tree limbs and set his sights back on the trail.

If Garrett hadn't been so concerned about getting caught and getting Emma to the cabin, he'd have laughed at the picture they must have made. To an unwary observer, the pair of horses picking their way stealthily up the mountain side mounted by masked riders in black would look like a page out of the annals of history—or a scene from *The James Boys Ride Again*.

He'd never seriously connected himself to the gene pool that had produced his notorious ancestors. Jesse had always been the one in the family to perpetuate the outlaw image. Still, what he was doing was so far afield from his nature, Garrett couldn't help but wonder if his connection to Frank and Jesse of old hadn't played a part in the actions he'd taken tonight.

It was too late to analyze now. He only hoped he hadn't wallowed around in self-pity for so long that it was too late to save his marriage.

They'd unloaded the horses an hour ago, leaving the truck hidden in a copse of trees, waiting for Jesse's return. Jesse led the way because Garrett hadn't wanted to scale the trail along the canyon rim by himself. Not when Emma's safety was at stake. While the risk was minimal in daylight, under cover of darkness the climb could get tricky.

This was territory all three James boys knew as well

as the faces that stared back at them in the mirror each morning. This section of the Wind River Range, with its craggy cliffs and restless wind was ingrained in their psyches. Their affinity for the mountain and the river was as elemental as speech, as basic as pride and honor. Wind River was the place they'd taken for granted as children. It was the place they'd played out their adolescent fantasies. They'd been mountain men here. They'd been outlaws. They'd lived by the Code of the West and ridden with the speed of the wind.

It was a place of memories and reflections—and it was the one place where they still returned to find their centers as men.

The best part of Garrett's past was here—and as they cleared the summit and began the descent to the valley where the roofline of a distant cabin separated itself from the shadows, he was risking everything on the hope that he'd find the best part of his future here, too.

Emma woke to a sweet breeze, birdsong and the mother of all headaches. Slowly she willed her eyes open—then stared in astonished wonder around her. Everywhere she looked, everything she touched was as alien as it was wonderful.

The comforter under which she slept was old and worn and snugly warm. The bed on which she lay was big and wide and as soft as downy feathers. Flowers— a fresh bouquet of wild irises, goldenrod and buttercups sat on an old oaken bedside table. Wonderful scents drifted in through the open window—clean mountain air, the earthy tang of pine, the brilliance of sunshine. From somewhere in what she'd decided could only be a cabin, the rich aroma of fresh-brewed coffee and frying bacon wafted on the air and sent her tummy rumbling.

Confused, disoriented, she pressed the pads of her fingertips against her throbbing temples, then stretched experimentally. Except for her head, she seemed to be fine—exhausted but fine—although the only thing familiar, she realized, as she resumed her study of her surroundings, was the white satin nightgown she was wearing.

Above her, open beams framed a vaulted ceiling made of rough-cut logs aged to a golden brown. The walls of what she had decided was a loft bedroom were constructed of the same coarse timbers. The austerity of the loft was broken only by a scattering of framed pictures—one of which was a photograph of two men that looked so old it could have been a tintype. She was trying to pin down why their faces looked vaguely familiar, when she heard the creak of weight on wood.

She jerked her head toward the sound—and saw Garrett standing there.

The sudden rumble of her heart intensified the pounding in her head.

His expression was guarded as he watched her from the top of the stairs that led to the loft and to the bed on which she lay.

A barrage of emotions tumbled through her, fast, fierce and varied. Confusion and disbelief, maybe even a hint of suspicion, tangled with an odd mix of anger and relief. But above them all she felt awareness. Of the look of him. Of the scent of him. Of a damnable wanting that hadn't died or even diminished after all this time.

She'd seen him like this hundreds of times: barefoot in blue jeans, a mug of coffee in his hand. His shirt had been hastily thrown on, hanging open to frame a broad chest heavily dusted with dark curls. The blue eyes that watched her were intense and brooding. The black hair she'd so ruthlessly shaved was almost back to its usual length and had been brushed through by the restless rake of his fingers.

He was virility personified, strength incarnate, innately sensual. And now, as always, he was so beautiful it made her chest hurt.

He'd been hers once. She'd known him once. She didn't know the man who watched her now. Just like she was beginning to think she didn't know who she was anymore—and that uncertainty had become far too recurrent a theme in her life. Now here she was, entrenched in a whole new set of unknowns.

Gathering the quilt to her breast, she eased herself up until she was propped against the headboard. She didn't know where she was, how she'd gotten here or why an anger that was both justified and warranted had less force than this aching awareness.

"How are you feeling?"

His voice was soft with concern, a gruffly velvet murmur that glided across her skin and made her shiver.

With wary anticipation, she watched as he walked to the bed and sat down a measured distance away. His open shirt not only showcased the tanned width of chest, but the washboard leanness of his belly, where dark curls thickened then delved below his navel and beyond.

With concerted effort she ignored his question, worked past her physical reactions and got right down to the heart of the matter. "What's going on, Garrett? Where's Sara?"

"Sara's fine," he assured her and offered her the coffee. She hesitated just long enough that he pressed the mug into her hands with a patient smile. "She's still with Maddie, and they both know you're with me."

He sounded so calm. So controlled. Both factors were typical of Garrett—and intimidating now, when she couldn't calm her thoughts long enough to figure out where she was or how she'd gotten here. Couldn't control her reactions when the simple shift of the bed beneath his weight turned her insides to warm knots of yearning.

She closed her eyes, searched through the cobwebs clogging her mind. With a groan she remembered the celebration Maddie had proposed they commemorate with a bottle of wine. That memory explained the headache. It also explained why she couldn't piece together more than misty, fragmented images: Garrett whispering to her in the night; the hum of an engine and the bump of the road; the pleasant scent of leather and horse; moonlight peeking through moving clouds and gently swaying pine boughs.

She let her head drop back against the pillow, willing it all together. "You—last night. You came to Maddie's. You brought me—" She made a vague gesture that encompassed the cabin and relayed her confusion. The return of the Southern drawl into her speech was telling of her uncertainty. "Here?" she deduced, struggling to regain her composure. "You brought me here from Maddie's?"

At his slow, confirming nod, she narrowed her brows. "I can't believe she'd willingly let you do that."

Though he made an effort to stall it, one corner of his mouth lifted with the slightest hint of a grin. "I wouldn't say she was willing, exactly, but she understood that her permission really didn't factor into this."

It took a moment for the implication to settle. When it did, so did an onslaught of memory. She set the coffee mug on the bedside table with a trembling hand, unable to mask her disbelief. "You…kidnapped me?"

He looked away, then back. "If you want to call it that."

Stunned, shaken, but unable to muster any real fear, she dragged the hair away from her face. "What else would you call it? How could you do that?" Disbelief overrode anger. Both colored her words, just as guilt colored his.

"You didn't leave me many options."

"My God…" Still at odds with what he'd done, she sat up straighter, suppressed a groan at the resurgence of pain pounding in her head. "I don't believe this."

"If it's any consolation, I'm having a little trouble believing it myself right about now." His smile this time was thoughtful, apologetic. "It was one of those it-seemed-like-a-good-idea-at-the-time sort of things."

Still in denial, she touched the flat of her hands to her temples as if to hold her head on. "What—were you drunk?"

"No." Though sheepish, his smile inched a little wider. "But fortunately for me you were or I don't think I could have pulled it off."

"Will you stop grinning? This is not funny."

His expressive face relayed both contrition and concern. "I'm hoping that someday it will be."

She shook her head—and immediately regretted it. Pain lanced behind her eyes. "It's never going to be funny. What it's going to be is over. I don't know what you're planning, Garrett, but whatever it is, it's going to happen without me. I want you to take me back to Jackson. Now."

She told herself it was anger, not fear that drove her. Nothing about Garrett caused her fear—not physically. But she still didn't want to be alone with him. More to the point, she couldn't afford to be alone with him. She felt too susceptible to everything about him that had made her love him. Too exposed to the emotions that he could kindle with a look or a smile, or the simple touch of his hand.

Anger wasn't just the weapon of choice. It was the only one she had against him. She made herself get a good grip on it. Then she wielded it like a club.

"Now, Garrett. I want you to take me back now."

He gave her a long, solemn look, then rose from the bed. Shoving his hands in his hip pockets, he walked to the window, leaned a shoulder against the wall and stared grimly outside. "We need to talk, Em. That's not going to happen back in Jackson."

When he turned toward her, no smile touched his mouth. Not a whisper of humor lit his eyes. "That's why I brought you here. To give us a few days alone and a clear chance to fix things between us."

There was no threat in his tone, just gentle determination. A fist squeezed tightly around her heart. She could deal with the determination but not the gentleness.

A weariness born of her pounding head and three months of heartache weighed down her shoulders. Still, she held her ground. "It's too late to fix anything."

"Maybe," he agreed after a long moment. "Maybe you're right. To tell you the truth, I don't know what to think anymore. But I do know that I want the chance to try. To have that chance, I had to get you alone.

"Look," he strode back to the bed and sat down again. Hitching a knee onto the mattress, he angled himself toward her. "I know that stealing you away in the night like this was crazy. I'm not particularly proud of my methods, but like I said, you didn't leave me many options. So I did what I felt I had to do.''

He was too close, too compelling, and he made it too easy for her to want to give in. She knew only one way to combat the urge to do just that. ''Then you'll understand when I tell you I have to do what I have to do. And that's get out of here.''

Panicked by his nearness and the effect it had on her, she threw back the covers, swung her feet to the floor and stood. Dizziness, in league with the pain, hit her hard and fast. She swayed, groped for something to hold on to—and found Garrett's hand. Strong. Steady. Supportive.

She tried to pull away, but her damn knees let her down. Just as they buckled, he scooped her up against him.

''Let go of me.'' Fighting him and the desire to let him enfold her in his strength and the comfort he offered, she pushed against his chest with her fists. ''I want to leave,'' she ground out with all the conviction she could muster.

''No.'' His eyes were suddenly as hard as the body pressed against her. ''You want to run.''

She opened her mouth to deny his accusation, but he cut her off with a truth she'd been denying even to herself.

''You want to run from this just like you ran away from our marriage.''

Garrett had been prepared for her anger. He hadn't planned on his own. Neither had he counted on this swift, hard surge of arousal. It hit him like a blast from a furnace as he held her in his arms.

The contact was an excruciatingly tactile reminder of

how much he missed her in his life—how much he
needed her in his bed. She was silken heat draped in
white satin. She was fragrant flesh and sensual woman,
as potent as wine to his senses, as provocative as sin to
his libido. And dammit, he wanted her back.

Last night when he'd sneaked into her room, he
hadn't been able to resist kissing her. When she'd
melted against him, he'd nearly drowned in the flood
of desire. Her instant, liquid response had told him
she'd wanted him with the need and the fire that had
been missing from their marriage even before she'd left
him. He could have taken her then.

He could take her now. Right now. And they both
knew it.

Every shivery breath she drew quivered with the
thready ache of arousal. Every heated inch of flesh
pressed against him pulsed with the fevered rush of passion.

He knew how to make her beg. Knew how to make
her cry out in pleasure then rescue her from the brink
of pain. He knew he could make her his again—if only
for this moment.

But a moment would never be enough, and that's all
he would gain if he pushed her too far too soon. She
needed more than physical release to heal the hurts
she'd been nursing. So did he. Now, more than ever, he
needed to remember that.

The unsteadiness of his hands gave away his struggle.
The longing in her eyes gave away hers. His sweet,
vulnerable Emma was as needy as he was. And as in-
censed by her body's response as she was panicked by
it.

With cautious control he let out a deep breath. With
deliberate care he loosened his hold. Her reaction to that

small concession was as volatile as a flash fire. She slammed her fist against his chest and tried to shove him away. He held her fast.

If it was a fight she wanted, she was going to get it—if for no other reason than to keep him from tumbling her back on the bed and plunging them both into the path of a need that grew stronger and more dangerous with every heartbeat.

"Listen to me. Listen to me," he demanded as she twisted and pushed against him.

She was no match for his physical strength. He used it to his advantage. Holding her easily but with care, he battered her with a steady barrage of words she didn't want to hear.

"You're running because you're afraid. But it's time to face it, Em. It's time to listen to the truth.

"You made a mistake. You made a mistake," he repeated more gently, willing her to admit it. "What you saw was a client coming on to me. Nothing more. I didn't encourage it. I didn't return it. I didn't sleep with her. And I think you know that—I can't believe you don't know that—but you're afraid. After what you did to me, you're afraid to own up to the truth."

She stilled. Her breath was labored, her breasts strained against the thin white gown she wore. Physically he may have overpowered her, but from beneath the curtain of chestnut hair falling over her face, she still fought him with her eyes.

For long moments he searched her face for some sign of concession. When she stubbornly held her silence, he eased his hold again. When she didn't fight him this time, he pressed his point. "Is that it, Em? You're wondering now if you were wrong?"

All the fight seemed to have left her. He caressed her

arms gently, then let her go and simply watched as she sank back down on the bed. Through the silence he sensed a slight lowering of her guard. Her posture gave her away. She was feeling exposed and cornered and more vulnerable than she wanted him to know. To combat it, she tucked her knees to her chest, linked her arms around them and lowered her head.

After a long hesitation he took a chance and sat down next to her. Enclosing her ankle with his hand, he squeezed it through the satin of her gown. The small intimacy was automatic on his part. A familiar gesture. A comforting touch. A gentle reassurance that had once been as natural between them as making love.

Once she'd have snuggled into the comfort zone he tried to create for her. Not today. Today she drew her foot away. The distance she created was as emotional as it was physical.

He immediately felt the loss.

When she raised her head, the look in her eyes told him she felt it, too.

"How do you think you're going to get away with this?"

Her voice was soft, but her tone was as cutting as scissors set to paper. Clearly she intended to avoid dealing with his conclusions and his questions.

Refusing to give up, he held the line. "How am I going to get away with this? I'm not sure I can. But with so much at stake how could I not give it a try?"

He forced himself to soften his tone. "How could I listen to Sara tell me that her mommy's never happy anymore and not want to take you away and change that? How could I see you—too thin, too pale, too weary—and not want to make what's wrong in your life right?

"How could I love you, Em?" He curled a finger under her chin and lifted her head so she had to look at him. "How could I love you and watch you hurting and not want to fix it?"

With everything in her, Emma fought to hang on to her anger. But his words and his touch struck like battering rams against her defenses. The aching warmth in his eyes melted through her resolve like torch set to steel.

It was too much. Too much wanting to believe him. Too much guilt over what she'd done to him. But overriding it all was the telling memory of another woman on the receiving end of a smile so intimate it should only have been hers. Only hers.

It was that memory that grounded her again. It was that memory that rallied the anger she needed to mask the hurt.

Oblivious to the tears leaking down her cheeks, she knotted her fingers around a fistful of quilt. "Damn you. Damn you for sounding so willing to fix things when you're the one who broke them."

Ignoring the ache in her chest, she threw his words back in his face. "You want to play *how could I?* Fine. I can play that game. Only let's change it to *how could you?* How could you say you love me and take another woman to your bed?"

Saying the words, watching his face darken at the accusation only added to her anguish. She swallowed back a far-too-familiar thickness clogging her throat.

"How could you do that to me and then lie about it? Did you expect me to just sit like a sorry little sparrow and pretend you were *working* all those nights when you came home late? And how could you possibly think that there could be any future for us with her between us?''

The cords in his neck tautened. His eyes grew hard. But his voice stayed calm—dangerously so. "How many ways can I say it? There is no her. There was no affair. There was nothing.''

She clenched the quilt tighter, damning herself for wanting to believe him, damning him for being so convincing.

"Do you know how badly I want to hit you right now? I'm not stupid. Don't treat me like I am. I know what I saw." A bitter laugh welled up. "She was all over you. You weren't backing away.''

The breath he drew was heavy, the muscle in his jaw clenched tight. "She was a client.''

"Oh, right. You mentioned that. Well." She waved a hand through the air. "That makes it all right, then, doesn't it?''

"No, dammit. I'm just trying to explain.''

"Fine. Explain then, if you weren't lovers, why she felt she could touch you that way. She was in your space, Garrett." Her words echoed in the pulsing silence that followed. "She was in *my* space," she added—pain, anger and humiliation lacing every word. "Only a woman who knows she's invited would make herself at home there.''

A flicker of guilt clouded his eyes then was gone. She hadn't realized how much blood that small, telling sign would draw. Hadn't acknowledged to herself until she saw it that a part of her was holding out hope that her accusations were unfounded.

"Okay." His reluctant affirmation relayed as much defiance as admission. A knife couldn't have sliced deeper. "So maybe I was sending out some signals,'' he went on, his eyes hard, his face grim, his tone clipped and defensive.

"Maybe after months of feeling you slowly pull away from me, watching you turn away from me in bed more often than you turned toward me, it was a turn-on that an attractive woman found me desirable."

Though guilt laced his words, the tension that had been building in her breast twisted so tight she could barely breathe. Yes, she had turned away from him, but no more than he'd turned away from her.

"And maybe I was hurting. Maybe I was tempted." His words jarred a defense already weakened by a sense of inadequacy. "I don't know. Maybe I was even flirting a little to boost my ego. But that's as far as it went. That's as far as it would ever go."

Even more than his words, she heard another message in his tone. When she could finally speak, the words came out on a raspy whisper. "So you're saying this is all my fault."

"No. Dammit no." He swore viciously. Then swore again. Dragging both hands roughly through his hair, he rose from the bed and stalked across the room. "I'm trying to be truthful with you," he ground out as he turned wearily back to face her. "You think I'm proud of myself? You think that it made me feel like a man to encourage her instead of discourage her when I knew it would never go anywhere? I was hurting, Em. And I was lonely." The anger bled back into his words just as the anguish darkened his face. "I was lonely," he repeated. "So lonely that for one second there, I told myself that if I did sleep with her, maybe I was justified."

His admission fell on her battered defenses like a lead weight. She covered her ears with her hands. She couldn't listen to this anymore. She couldn't think past his words, couldn't hear past the voice of guilt she'd lived and breathed for longer than she wanted to remember. "I don't want to hear any more."

But she couldn't stop the thoughts from swelling. And for the first time she felt real fear as the words that welled up inside her knotted in her chest and clogged her throat. She tried desperately to swallow them back. But they were too strong, too painful to keep inside any longer. They spilled like blood, trailed like tears, escaping with an ache so strong it stole her breath.

"Emma—"

"No. Don't say another word." Panic was a piece of jagged glass cutting huge slashing wounds inside her. She struck out against it and because it frightened her so, she struck out against him.

"I don't want to listen to you twist things around until this is all my fault. I won't let that happen. Not to me. I won't let you do to me what my father did to my mother. And I sure as hell won't let you turn me into her!"

The electric edge of pain in her words split the air like lightning.

Stunned silence settled like a storm cloud in their wake.

Until this moment, until this wrenching moment of truth, she'd hadn't known. Had never suspected that the core of the fear she harbored was rooted in the shambles of her mother's life.

The tension in the loft vibrated with the concussion of a revelation so explosive it slammed the breath from her lungs.

"Oh, my God," she whispered, the aftershock of her admission rocking her. "My God," she murmured again and, defeated by the knowledge, lowered her face to her hands.

Garrett watched the color bleed from her face. Felt it rise in his own. He should have known. He should have seen or suspected the cause of the fear she'd been fighting.

He knew her mother's story. The dutiful wife, the soft-spoken, Southern socialite, Viola DuPree had left Mississippi and everything she'd known to follow her husband to Jackson all those years ago. In her determination to maintain their marriage, she'd accepted his lies even when faced with evidence of his repeated affairs. She'd done everything for him, lived her life for him, given up her dignity and pride for him—only to have him divorce her six months after they'd resettled in Wyoming and move in with the woman he'd uprooted his family to be near.

Viola's devastation had been complete. The waste, shameful. Once a vibrant, loving woman, she'd turned to prescription-induced oblivion, where the pain of depression neither touched nor tempered her life.

Clearly, though, it had touched Emma's. This beautiful, proud woman who was Viola's daughter was afraid the same thing was happening to her. Her father had destroyed her mother. He'd turned her into a victim. And now, imagined sin or real, Emma was pinning her father's crimes on him.

"Emma? Sweetheart." He touched a hand to her hair, stroked it gently. "Is that what this is all about?"

Her eyes were filled with the shock of discovery and a wild, consuming fear as she searched his face. He was certain she wasn't aware that she'd begun to cry. Soft, choked little sobs broke from her throat until she began weeping freely. His heart breaking for her, he pulled her into his arms and held her.

The fight deserted her completely. She clung to him, turned to him as she had when they'd been young lovers and she'd poured out her hurt and her fears.

She cried for her mother. She cried for herself. And even though she didn't say it, he knew she also cried for the demise of everything they'd lost.

When she had no tears left to shed, Garrett brushed the hair away from her face.

"I love your mother, Em. I know you love her, too. But you are not her," he whispered, cupping her face in his hands. "You could never be anything like her. And I'm not him. I could never do to you what your father did to her."

He pressed his lips to her brow. "Think about that. Think about it, and you'll know."

For a long moment, he just sat with her, neither expecting nor receiving a response, only wondering how they had let a breach this wide wedge its way between them. And agonizing over how, with so much misunderstanding clouding the view, they were possibly going to see the way back to each other.

Weary with the questions and the causes, he pried her carefully away from him. With the gentleness of a father soothing a child, he lowered her back down to the bed.

"I know we've got problems, Em," he whispered as he eased the covers up to her chin. "I've known it for a long time, but please, please believe me when I tell you that another woman isn't one of them."

She closed her tear-swollen eyes and turned her head on the pillow.

"There's only been one woman for me. Ever. And I

need her. I need her to help me find the way through this mess. Please say you'll stay with me. Just…just give it a week to see if we can figure this out.''

He didn't know what else to do. Didn't know what else to say. And even now that he finally understood the root of her doubts, he didn't know if he would ever completely comprehend what he'd done to make her lose her trust in him.

Feeling as defeated and as weary as she looked, he trailed the back of his fingers across her brow. With a diminishing hope that the healing would ever begin, he gave her shoulder a gentle squeeze.

"Rest for a while. Just rest," he repeated on a husky whisper and rose from the bed. "You'll find some clothes in the chest under the window when you feel like getting dressed. When you come downstairs, we'll talk."

For a long moment he stood at the top of the stairs waiting for something that never came. She didn't call out to him. She didn't ask him to stay. She just turned her face to the wall and let him walk away.

He hadn't been aware that he'd been holding his breath until his chest began to ache from the weight of it. He let it out slowly—then did the only thing he felt she wanted him to do.

He left her. Alone with her doubts. Alone with her fears. Just as he was alone with her tears still damp on his shirt.

Five

After he left her in the loft, Garrett walked out to the wraparound deck. Settling deep in a willow chair with his bare feet crossed at the ankles and propped on the deck rail, he wrestled with a weariness that had seeped into his blood like sludge.

He'd been so sure that if he could get her alone, he could fix things between them. But even with the revelations the last hour had unearthed—maybe even because of them—he wasn't sure any longer.

He was afraid for her. And that made him afraid for them.

Fatigue eventually caught up with him. It had been a long, tense night. Discounting that, he'd been working extralong hours at the office and on the sites of several projects the past few weeks while he'd set his plan in motion. What little free time he'd had, he'd spent hauling up supplies and getting the cabin ready for Emma.

It had been a long time since anyone had spent any time here—longer still since a woman had been in-residence.

He fell asleep wondering if she would insist that he take her back to Jackson after she'd rested. Wondering what he'd do if she did. He woke troubled by the same thought—and by a sense that he was no longer alone.

Sitting up slowly, he scrubbed a hand over his face, rolled the stiffness out of his shoulders and turned to see her standing there.

She was dressed in the new jeans and yellow cotton knit sweater he'd bought her. Her feet were covered in the buttery soft doeskin moccasins he'd known she would like. She'd brushed her long hair until it shone, then pulled it back from her face with one of the gold clips he'd left for her on the dresser.

Though her eyes were still a little puffy, she looked rested and sleep soft. Despite her loss of weight and the lack of color in her cheeks, he was still, and would always be, electrified by her beauty. What he saw in her eyes, however, had the most profound effect on him. She was still struggling with her decision—and that meant she was still afraid.

Ignoring the sinking feeling in his gut, he rose and studied her profile. She leaned against a porch post. Clutching it with both hands, she pressed her cheek against the sturdy rough timber and looked over the valley. Her silence could mean anything from resistance to reluctance to reminiscence.

"Did you rest?" he asked inanely.

She nodded. "It's been a long time since I've slept that soundly."

"You must have needed it." Another lame, innocuous comment.

They both recognized the wordplay for what it was.

Evasion. Neither of them was willing to be the first to tread the path that would lead them to the heart of the matter.

She glanced at him over her shoulder, then averted her gaze back to the river where its mad scramble over rock and stone fifty yards away created ribbons of undulating silver and frothy lace. On the far bank, lodgepole pine and quaking aspen climbed gently sloping foothills that abruptly gave way to soaring, snowcapped peaks.

"It's beautiful here." It was a simple truth, yet another not-so-simple diversion.

His heart rose to his throat in anticipation. "Aside from the isolation, the beauty is part of what made me decide to bring you here. An added enticement I'd hoped would help you decide to stay with me. I guess the question now is, did it work?"

Finally it was out. They both knew the beauty of the Wind River Valley had little to do with her decision— just as they both knew everything was riding on her answer.

She was silent for too long. Too long to keep his hands from sweating. Too long to stall a broken breath.

"Ten years, Em," he reminded her, then made what he told himself would be his last pitch. "It should count for something. It should be worth a week. One week. Can't we give ourselves seven days to see if there's anything to salvage?"

When she turned to him, her eyes were troubled, the hands she cupped around her elbows slightly trembling.

"And what if there isn't? What if there's nothing left to piece together?"

It was his turn to look out over the valley. His turn to clench unsteady hands over the split-log porch rail and hang on. "Then at least we'll both leave here knowing we tried."

Moments slogged by. Somewhere in the distance a raven called. The wind whispered through the pines. The river snaked through an ageless path carved from earth and stone. The endless, boundless sounds of the valley all registered on a peripheral level. So did the sound of his own breathing, the heavy beat of his heart. Until he heard his name.

"Garrett."

He turned his head. Straightening in slow motion, he looked from her face to the hand she offered.

She was hesitant, but she was reaching out. Of more significance, she was reaching out to him. For the first time since this all started, he saw something in her eyes that translated to hope.

He pushed away from the rail. Enclosing her small hand in his, he brought it to his lips.

"You'll stay?"

For long moments she said nothing as she sifted through the emotions the past several hours had kindled.

"Em?" he prompted when he couldn't stand it any longer.

Slowly she met his eyes. Slower still, she searched his face. "I'll stay."

If relief had been sweeter, he would have overdosed on it. If hope had been higher, he'd have taken wing. He wanted to take her in his arms and carry her to his bed and love all their problems away.

But she was as fragile as glass standing there. Still hesitant. Still unsure even as she agreed to take this to another level.

Reining in his excitement, he approached her as he would a skittish colt, with patience and with care. "This is a good decision you've made. I'll do everything I can to make sure you're not sorry."

For an instant, for an eternity, their eyes met and held, and then she moved into his arms.

The same desperation that had compelled him to bring her here in the dark of night had him burying his fingers in her hair and drawing her close.

"We're going to work this out." He lowered his mouth to the top of her head, fighting a welling of emotion so strong it stung his eyes and thickened his throat. "That's what this week is all about. We're going to figure out what went wrong, and then we're going to fix it."

Urging her gently away, he cupped her slim shoulders in his palms and spoke from his heart. "I want you back. You. The woman I married. A woman who is strong and loving, a woman who knows her own mind and isn't afraid to speak it. A woman who stands up for what she believes and faces her problems head-on."

"And what if that woman's gone?" There was fear there. Fear and desperation. "What if she's been replaced by some maniac who goes off the deep end and drugs the father of her child? What if that woman no longer knows what she wants or who she is?"

Her soulful brown eyes met his with equal measures of despair and doubt—both so profound, he physically felt her struggle.

"Then we'll find her. Here. Together." He squeezed her shoulders, a gesture of confidence, an expression of hope. "And we'll find out what went wrong. I let you down, Em. I know that—but not in the way you think.

"I won't lie and say it hasn't been hard—knowing that it was easier for you to believe I'd been unfaithful than to deal with whatever else our problems are. But we'll work through that.''

He willed the right words to come. "I've made mistakes. We both have. But I'm not playing games when I say I don't know what they were. That's what we need to work on. Before we can, you've got to believe that there's one mistake I've never made—never wanted to. There's never been anyone else. Never.''

She closed her eyes, swallowed hard.

"Give me the chance to make you trust me again. Give *us* the chance to trust each other.''

"And if we can't?''

He'd weighed his response to that question a hundred times in his mind. It took all his strength of will to voice it. "Then I'll sign the divorce papers if you still want me to,'' he said finally.

She'd never been able to hide her feelings from him. Her eyes gave her away every time. Right now they were telling him she was scared and about two deep breaths away from changing her mind.

He wasn't going to let that happen. And to make sure it didn't, he knew he had to take it slow and easy. This pact they'd made was very fragile. Her feelings were still too raw, too exposed, to explore in depth—not just yet. For that matter, so were his.

Recognizing that, he decided to proceed with caution, give them both a little room. For the time being, it only made sense that they'd both be more comfortable dealing with the mundane. And for now, that was enough for him. Just knowing she was going to stay was enough to raise his spirits to a level he hadn't thought he'd ever feel again.

"You missed breakfast—and lunch,'' he said with a soft smile meant to set her at ease and let her know he wouldn't crowd her. "How about we take care of that first?"

When she cautiously returned his smile, he knew he was reading her right.

Without another word he walked to the door and held it open for her. After a slight hesitation she walked through.

The simple act shouldn't have held as much weight as it did. They both recognized, however, that it was as symbolic as it was physical. He'd opened a door; she'd walked through it—not just physically but emotionally. His hope grew with his anticipation as she allowed him to place a light hand at the small of her back and steer her toward the kitchen.

Emma let him sit her down at a rough-hewn pine table, then watched on as he dug around in the fridge for the makings for sandwiches.

An overwhelming flood of emotions swamped her. One of them was discovery. She'd found out a lot about herself this morning. It was scary and a little humbling to know she'd been harboring the fear that her marriage might mirror the disaster her mother's had been. It was also painfully enlightening—and she still had to figure out how to deal with what that closeted fear had done not only to her but to Garrett and ultimately to Sara.

Aside from that, though, relief suddenly—and surprisingly—overrode her regrets and uncertainties. She'd made a decision—the first one that had felt right since the night she'd left Garrett. Whatever happened over the next several days, whatever the outcome, she'd at least find some peace in knowing she had given it a try.

Relief came from another quarter, as well. Now that she thought about it, ever since she'd seen Garrett standing at the top of the loft steps, a sense of safety had worked to erode her anger. In her head she knew she should be outraged with him for kidnapping her. But in truth the knowledge that he cared so much that he'd swept her away like a thief in the night had warmed a part of her heart that had been cold for a very long time. She gave herself a little dispensation on that count.

Was any woman truly immune to the fantasy of being swept away by a dominant male who had risked everything to have her to himself? Especially a male who was as beautiful as this one? The right look, the right touch, and she was in danger of falling into his arms and into the oblivion she sought in his loving.

After all these months of missing him, it was tempting. *He* was tempting as he moved on bare feet, his jeans hugging his slim hips. He still had the body of an athlete. Had always had the look of an outlaw—all the James boys did—with his dark hair tumbling recklessly over his forehead and eyes that could cloud over with the deep blue of a summer storm, or liquefy to the hazy mist of a distant fog.

The hands that made their sandwiches were big. They were rugged hands, working man's hands that could be filled with strength, tempered to an uncommon gentleness or heated to sensual roughness. Memories of those hands on her body sent an erotic little shiver rippling down her spine—along with a wake-up call.

She was straying back into dangerous territory. Satisfying physical wants and needs would solve nothing between them. Their problems ran deeper than that. And they had miles to go toward resolving them—*if* they could resolve them.

The moment called for caution. In fact, it called for information and a safe topic of discussion.

"Are you ever going to get around to telling me where we are?"

Her question brought his head around. He studied her face to test her mood, then, reading it right, relaxed into a grin that was engagingly crooked and just a little coy.

Too quickly, too easily, her own reaction came. Despite her resolve to keep her feelings in check, she couldn't stall a return smile when his dancing eyes met hers. She'd missed that grin. She'd missed him.

"Got any guesses?"

She shrugged, considered, shook her head. "We're not in the Tetons."

"You've got that right. We're in the Wind River Range."

"Wind River?" She took another long, slow look around her as the significance of the location struck her. "Then this would be the cabin. *The* cabin," she repeated, fairly stunned by the realization. "Which means I'm on hallowed ground."

He chuckled at the staged reverence in her voice. The James boys had made no bones over the years that they considered the cabin their father had built in the valley an exclusively male domain. Except for their mother, no woman had ever crossed the threshold.

"Haven't you broken some sacred covenant by bringing me here?"

Before he could answer, another thought struck her. She wrinkled her brow. "I thought the only way into the valley was on foot or by horseba—" She let her sentence trail off when she realized the implication. "You brought me here by horseback and I didn't even know it?"

He scratched the stubble that darkened his jaw. "You've never been a drinker, Em. I guess now we both know why.'' Compassion and a hint of humor touched his eyes. "How is the head by the way?"

His compassion resurrected a guilt she'd been struggling with since she'd left him and broke the easiness of the mood. It took a moment, but she gathered her courage and broached a subject she felt compelled to face. "Better than yours, I'd suspect, the morning after...the morning after I left you."

Remorse for the grotesqueness of the sins she'd committed against him swelled to an awareness so huge it filled her chest to bursting. She'd drugged him. She'd shaved his head. She'd torn his life apart and deprived him of his child—all because of her own insecurities.

Yes, their marriage had been in trouble. And yes, seeing him with that woman that day had been painful and shocking, but it hadn't given her license to do what she'd done.

She looked at her hands. "I'm...I'm so sorry for what I did to you. I...I still can't believe I—"

"Hey—let's not think about that right now." The firmness in his tone stopped her and brought her head up. Though his voice was hard, his eyes were gentle. "We've got all week. Let's just ease into this, okay?"

She realized immediately that putting off that particular discussion was his way of protecting her. Protecting her had always been one of the things Garrett did best. Letting him, was one of her weaknesses. He'd always had a need to make her feel safe. She realized—to his credit and her shame—that she'd had an answering need to let him. He'd always been so strong and so willing to cloak her in that strength. She suspected now, that her willingness to let him may have contributed to the mess they were in.

But this shouldn't be about his strength, she thought

dismally. It should be about hers. And hers was at an all-time low.

That had to change.

If they were to have any chance of fixing all the wrongs between them, she was going to have to come to terms with her weaknesses.

He was offering her the time to accomplish that—recognizing before she did that what she needed most right now was time.

With a hesitant nod, she agreed. They would have to deal with their feelings about what she'd done to him. There were a lot of things they had to deal with. But it wouldn't be today. Today they'd get used to being together again.

The silence, however, still hung too heavy with her memory of that day. To shake it, she averted her gaze from his and visually explored her surroundings.

"It's quite impressive." A lift of her hand encompassed the cabin. "I've always had a curiosity about it. Never figured I'd actually get to see it—not the way you boys guarded its location."

Sending her a soft smile, he set the bacon he'd fried earlier along with lettuce, tomatoes and bread on the counter. He lifted the coffeepot in invitation. At her nod he pulled out two mugs and filled them.

"Some things are just a little hard to let go of, you know?" He made a lazy, sweeping gaze of the chinked log walls, vaulted ceilings and masculine, rustic furnishings.

"This place has always had a special significance for us. Dad built it. We claimed it as a for-men-only sanctuary—even when we were just boys pretending to be men."

A wealth of memories warmed his eyes. For a moment she could see they had transported him back to another time.

"Then I guess I should feel honored that I'm here," she said softly, feeling as though she was intruding on his thoughts.

He only smiled. "Under the circumstances, I'd say honored is a generous attitude."

He hadn't meant to but he'd given her another opening to talk about the very topic he wanted to avoid. The fact that she didn't follow through was a measure of how right he'd been to avoid it for the time being. She wasn't ready, and she was grateful that he had recognized it.

"And how do your brothers feel about me being here?" she asked instead. "They were in on this, weren't they?" she surmised when a slow, secret smile deepened the creases in his cheeks. "I should have known. The James boys always stick together."

"Even at the risk of being charged with kidnapping," he added as he built their sandwiches.

That notion prompted another—the one she'd been worried about. "My mother—she's bound to go a little 'taz' over this."

He set a plate in front of her, took a chair on the opposite side of the table and tucked into his sandwich. "Jesse's taking care of that."

"Taking care?"

"To set her at ease. Your mother's always been a sucker for Jess. A little choirboy grinning, some 'aw shucks, ma'am' posturing and he'll charm the socks off her—and in the process, hopefully he'll convince her you're fine and in good hands."

She picked up her own sandwich, picturing Jesse with her mother. "That ought to be a good trick."

He flashed a quick, confident grin. "I have faith that he's well motivated. According to Jess, he's much too pretty to go to prison and become the significant other of someone named Ivan for the next twenty years."

In spite of the seriousness of the situation, she had to smile. Too soon, however, concern edged out her amusement.

"What about *your* mother?"

Serious now, he rested his forearms on the table. "She said to tell you that she loves you, asked that you forgive her for sanctioning this—and she hopes you like the lingerie she picked out."

Garrett watched as color spread across her cheeks. He immediately sensed what had caused it. He'd seen the lingerie. He wanted to see her in it. And out of it.

Icing the thought, he dug back into his sandwich to keep his mind from wandering somewhere it had no place going—not yet.

She took a delicate bite then chewed thoughtfully. "I still don't know how you got past Maddie."

"That was Clay's job."

"Another intriguing prospect."

"And then some," he agreed.

When she grinned again, he knew she was finally relaxing. "When I left with you last night, she was winding up to call him everything but a child of God."

Her smile leveled then faded. "She means well, Garrett."

"I know. Look," he said, sensing that they were close to stumbling into that quicksand they were trying to skirt. "I want to propose something."

Propping both elbows on the table, he waited until she gave him her full attention.

"We've got problems, Em. But we've got a past together, too. A good one. That day in the park—I asked you to tell me you didn't love me. You didn't do it. I chose to believe then that it meant you couldn't do it. And even though I don't expect you to say it, I choose to believe it now."

He reached across the table, enfolded her hands with his. When she let him, he pressed on. "I love you, Em. I've never stopped loving you. In the next few days I want to remind you of that—and to try to recapture what we had together."

"Garrett—"

"No, wait. Let me say this while I've got the words together. It's too hard right now. It's too hard for both of us to analyze what went wrong. So let's not start there. Let's start with what went right. We've both lost so much the past few months. Let's take a few days to remember what we had and let that work for us to get it back."

Her eyes were sad as they focused on their joined hands. "Going back isn't going to solve anything."

"Maybe not," he conceded. "But for now—just for now—I think it's what we need. We need to get grounded again. We need some time to heal a bit before either one of us is strong enough to tackle the things that need to be fixed."

She didn't say anything. But she didn't withdraw her hands, either. He stroked the back of her knuckles. Felt the moment when the fight went out of her and the compliance eased in.

"How do we do that?" Her voice was soft, wistful with longing. "How do we go back?"

He squeezed her hands, then sank back in his chair with a smile. "You let me worry about that, okay?"

Her expression relayed both confusion and curiosity,

and just a spark of excitement that sent his pulse sky-rocketing. They'd begun. And he liked the sound of that beginning far more than the sound of an end.

His appetite suddenly ravenous, he polished off his sandwich, then watched with pleasure as she did the same with hers.

Jonathan James had built the cabin in the Wind River Valley as a retreat for himself and his bride. But as their family expanded and the boys had grown in size and activity, the cabin had become more theirs than their parents'.

Jonathan had brought them here for long weekends throughout their youth, and the brothers had gradually staked their claim to it and the land encompassing it. Garrett, Clay and Jesse still spent time here—either together or alone—as men.

Not that a little recent "spiffing up" hadn't made it habitable for a woman, too. With Logan's help—who'd turned out to be a closet romantic and a bit of an outlaw himself—Garrett had stocked food, refired the generator so they'd have electricity, run a line to the river so they'd have water and cleaned until the windows shone and the appliances sparkled. He'd even bought new sheets for the loft bed, and after a lengthy self-debate, hauled up the necessities to set the mood to make Emma his again.

And now here they were, in this place that was both special and magical, and he hoped to hell he didn't blow it.

After lunch he took her on a quick tour of the cabin, which basically consisted of the loft above and one large great room below that served as living room, dining room and kitchen. A small but well-equipped bathroom and a dorm-style bedroom that the boys used to bunk in finished out the interior. They ended the tour on the wraparound, covered porch that offered multiple and equally breathtaking views of the valley.

"What would you like to do? This time is yours, Em."

Part of his plan was for her to rest here. He couldn't help but feel that above all else, rest was what she needed.

"I brought books." He rattled off a list of authors he'd known were her favorites. "And CDs." Again he'd made his selections with special attention to her taste in music, which ranged from classical to country with some contemporary pop mixed in for good measure.

Her smile thanked him, but her eyes were on the river. "It's a beautiful day. I think I'd like to walk."

He hesitated, then finally extended another overture of reconciliation on this cautious journey they were taking. "Do you want to walk alone, or would you like some company?"

Telling herself she'd been alone with her solitude and her thoughts for too long, Emma answered with a careful smile. "Company would be nice."

Cognizant of his silent support by her side, they explored the valley and the abundance of beauty it offered.

The valley was wide here, the forest a gradually thickening border. Aspen and pines of verdant green surrounded the meadow grass and scattering of nodding wildflowers like a living framework. She couldn't remember how long it had been since she'd let herself enjoy something so simple as sunshine. How long it had been since she had "played" outside the boundaries of doubt and pain.

She'd done little more than exist for the past three months. That's all she'd had the strength to do. But today due to the most unlikely of catalysts—the man who was responsible for her little descent into the abyss—she let herself feel: the kiss of the breeze on her face; its intimate caress as it lifted and played with her hair; the warmth of the sun on her nose as she tipped her face to the sky; the rustle of limbs and pine needles snapping beneath her feet.

Life. She'd missed it. She'd craved it.

She let him take her hand as they climbed over a downed tree trunk. She smiled when he picked her flowers and tucked them in her hair. With gentle words and winning smiles, he shared his valley and, in the process, invited her to make it hers as well.

He set the pace, and it was easy. Easy to claim this little pocket of heaven, easy to shut out regrets, to waylay fears. Easy to look at the man she'd fallen in love with and wish for a future as harmonious as the songs of the river and the rhythms of the wind.

It was ironic that it was Garrett—the man who had dragged her into darkness—who offered her the light. Yet at the moment she couldn't think of anyone else she would want to show her the way back.

Six

From its inception, Garrett's strategy had been to bring her here to court her. Their afternoon together had been an encouraging start. She'd softened. She'd smiled. She'd relaxed that guarded look and lost her focus on what had gotten them to this rocky point.

And when, toward twilight, he found her resting in a willow chair soaking up the last rays of the setting sun, he decided to slowly escalate his plan.

"You're looking very comfortable there, Emmy Lou. And prettier than the sunset."

To his delight she warmed to the mischief in his mood and conjured a little of her own. "You haven't called me Emmy Lou since I was sixteen and you were trying to unsnap my bra in the back seat of your car."

He winced, both penitent and amused. "I don't suppose I could convince you to be a little less selective with your memory."

The soft smile she gave him restored his faith in romance and in the pleasing power of hope.

"Why don't you try again, and we'll see what happens."

He eased a hip onto the porch rail. The sun was warm on his back. It painted a rosy blush on her cheeks, sent a slow-moving river of desire coursing through him. "Do you remember the first time I asked you to go out with me?"

She settled back, looking both comfy and coy as she laced her fingers over her middle. "I don't remember you *asking,* exactly. If I recall, it was more like, 'There's a good movie playing downtown. You could go with me if you want to.'"

He dropped his chin to his chest and groaned. "The last of the great romantics."

She shrugged, her wistful look telling him she was sifting through a few memories of her own. "You didn't do so bad. I remember you held the theater door open for me. I thought that was pretty romantic."

He grunted. "Much as I hate to admit it, that probably had more to do with fear than romance—if I hadn't minded my manners and one of my mother's friends had seen me, it would have gotten back to her. It always did. And she'd have hung me out to dry."

"Ah, so you were only playing the role of a gentleman."

"To win that slow Southern smile? Absolutely. At first, anyway." Charmed by the smile in question, he held her gaze. "But then—then there was just something about you that made me want to do things for you. Open doors, buy you flowers...leap tall buildings with a single bound."

She rose to stand beside him at the railing. "Which,

according to half the girls in the senior class, you could have done if you'd put your mind to it.''

He tried one of Jesse's "aw shucks" grins.

"A lowly little underclassman like me just went all atwitter every time you shot me one of those 'Hey, baby' smiles."

"'Hey baby' smiles?" He shuddered. "This is getting painful. What a jerk. Why did you even go out with me?''

It was her turn to grin. "It was the movie. I'd been wanting to see it all summer.''

He nodded sagely. "Obviously it wasn't my irrepressible charm.''

"Oh, you had plenty of that, too—when you weren't practicing your machismo.''

She eased a hip onto the rail, clearly enjoying his discomfort and the playful stroll down memory lane. "And then there was your other smile—the one you hadn't perfected as a come-on. Yes,'' she said, her eyes softening when his mouth twitched at the corners. "That's the one. That's the smile that talked me into saying yes.''

His eyes met hers with gentle entreaty. "What do you think the chances are of it working again—tonight?''

A sudden unease strung the tension back in her shoulders. He understood that. She thought he was asking for more. And he wanted to. But it was too soon. On that, he wanted to be clear.

"We're starting over, remember? From square one. All I want is a date. And this time I'm asking. Would you like to go to a movie with me tonight, Emma DuPree?''

Visibly relaxing, she shot a cursory glance over the valley, the abundance of trees, the total lack of civilization. "A movie? And just exactly where would we find a movie playing out here?"

"That's where a little bit of faith comes in," he murmured and extended his hand. "Trust me."

Her hesitation was brief and, he thought, telling when she placed her hand in his. He squeezed her fingers.

Little by little she was letting herself trust him again. Little by little he was going to reward that trust with truths.

"The lady wants to see a movie—I'm taking her to a movie. Stay here. I'll be right back."

Garrett and Logan had made no less than ten trips up and down the mountain on horseback preparing for this week. They'd lugged food and wine and gas for the generator. Garrett had personally wrestled with the books, the CD player and finally the TV/VCR combo he'd almost lost to a large boulder and a skittish mare. But the effort had been worth every bone-jarring, vertebrae-crunching ride, he decided when he led her into the cabin a few minutes later.

Her wondrous smile said it all. It also asked and answered the question hovering in her eyes. *Yes. He'd done it for her.* And he'd do it again in a heartbeat to see that look on her face.

Settling her onto the sofa, he loaded her down with popcorn, soda, and an outrageous assortment of movie theater candy.

"Now this definitely rings a few bells." Balancing her soda between her knees, she worked on the box of Milk Duds he'd asked her to open. "You bought all of this stuff on our first date, too."

"Because I wanted to impress you."

"And here I thought you were just a glutton."

He let out a long puff of air. "I was missing on every cylinder, wasn't I?"

"Not missing, exactly." Her brown eyes teased and tantalized. "Just misfiring a little. I thought it was cute."

"And I thought you smelled sweeter than any flower."

She laughed, a carefree spontaneous sound as she wrestled with the big bowl of buttery popcorn and finally settled for setting it on her lap.

"That's because you were used to locker-room smells. And because I'd been so nervous I'd spilled half a bottle of Gardenia on my sweater. I didn't think I was ever going to get the smell out."

"Your sweater," he echoed, lost in a young man's dream of perfection as the opening credits rolled. "You were something in that sweater. Do you know how many times I 'accidentally' brushed your breast with my arm on the pretense of reaching for the popcorn?"

"Twenty-seven."

When he slumped down farther in the sofa, she laughed.

"This is such a comedown—to find out all my smooth moves were as transparent as—Em?" He broke off when she became suddenly still. "What's wrong?"

"Nothing. Nothing's wrong." He followed the track of her gaze to the TV/VCR where the tape was rolling.

"How did you find this movie?" Her expression was soft, her eyes tender as she turned to him. "I...didn't think you remembered. I didn't think you liked it."

"What I liked was being with you. And how could I not remember? It's your favorite."

Emma couldn't say anything. Didn't trust herself to. His thoughtfulness was touching. The lengths he'd gone to, to find the movie, to set the mood, sparked all kinds of sensations. Her chest felt heavy and full. Her heart picked up an extra beat then steadied into a slow, rich rhythm.

She was so taken with the movie, so taken with him, that she let him transport her there—to that place in the past when their love was young and thrilling and new.

The transition was easy. He made it so as they sat side by side, almost touching, tingling with the need to touch.

He reached for the popcorn the same time she did. Their fingers bumped, brushed, drew slowly apart. Delicious little sparks, as electric and vibrant as the first time, left them wanting and wondering about more.

For long moments they watched the movie in silence. For longer moments she wondered when he'd make his move. And just like on that first date all those years ago, she wondered what she'd do when he did.

The anticipation built until she was aware of every breath he drew, of every subtle shift of his hip, the evenness of his breath in the darkness, the dark, musky scent of his skin.

She wanted to laugh at herself for her sophomoric expectancy. She wasn't a young girl, curious for the first taste of his lips. She was a woman who had known the wonder of this man's kisses. Yet it was that knowledge that made the anticipation so sweet. And so dangerously alluring.

When he finally raised his arms over his head in the pretense of a stretch, she almost bolted off the sofa. She answered his questioning frown with a self-conscious smile and a slight shake of her head.

"If I remember right," he whispered, stirring the fine

hair at her temple and firing the pulse at her throat, "the old move starts out something like this."

With a great show of nonchalance, he carefully lowered his arm across the back of the sofa.

"Step two," he continued, smoothing the edge of expectancy with a slow smile, "strategically, and so slowly so as not to be noticed, the arm descends down the back of the seat until…"

"Until?" she prompted, a little breathless, a little giddy when he paused dramatically.

"Until—and this is the part where the real finesse comes in—it's time to engage the decoy."

"Decoy?" Even his grin couldn't dull the sharpness of the sexual tension his nearness created.

"An innocent smile—" he demonstrated engagingly "—a subtle lean toward the popcorn—" again, he acted out his steps "—and by the time the lean is over, the arm is firmly settled on unsuspecting shoulders."

Even as she tried to match his playful smile, her voice went rusty and low. "Quite a maneuver. I…I had no idea of the tactical expertise required."

His gaze drifted to her mouth, lingered. "Very technical choreography."

Whatever lightness left in the moment was lost, steamrollered into nonexistence by a delicious, aching expectancy. Another mood, rimmed with sexual tension, brimming with awareness of their nearness, resurfaced and edged it out. He wanted to kiss her. And if he tried, she knew she would let him.

Her breath shimmered out. Her heart, already in jeopardy of overload, picked up an extra beat. And beside her, his blue eyes turned dark and dangerous.

He leaned toward her, cupped her jaw in his hand

and, at the last moment, wrenched his attention back to the movie.

Several moments passed before she realized she was holding her breath—several more before she managed to let it out. More still before she could establish a pattern of breaths she didn't have to think about.

She wasn't sure if she'd just been rescued from a dangerous fall, or left dangling by her fingernails from the edge of a mile high cliff.

With great difficulty she tried to follow his lead. She tried to relax. She even tried to be grateful for his restraint, but frustration blended with disappointment just the same.

It was later—much later—when a smile finally crept up on her. He truly was an outlaw—and he'd accomplished exactly what he'd set out to do. His arm was quite naturally draped over her shoulders—and she was snuggled easily against his warmth.

"This is nice," he murmured, pressing his mouth to her hair.

"Yes," she echoed, steeped again in the easy mood he'd created. "This is very nice."

By the time the final credits rolled, they'd polished off the popcorn and even a little of the candy. And the simple act of sharing a movie together in the dark had taken them a long way toward renewing the bond that had once held them together.

Like on their first date, Emma found herself wishing the night would never end. But like all good things, it had to.

She sensed his reluctance, too, when he rose, then held out his hand to help her up.

There were less than ten steps from the sofa to the

loft stairs. She counted every one, as with their hands linked, he slowly led her there.

"Do you remember how we ended our first date?" His question came out on a gruff whisper as he urged her up to the bottom step so their eyes were on a level.

"I remember everything about it," she answered with the same husky resonance.

"My heart beat then just like it's beating now." He brought her hand to his chest, held it there.

Beneath her palm, his pulse hammered hard and full and heavy.

His excitement made her breathless. "Mine, too."

Silence whispered, time ceased as his blue eyes held hers captive in the moment and the memories.

"Can I kiss you, Em? Like I did that night in the moonlight on your front porch?"

She blinked once, slowly, then with rapt fascination, averted her gaze to the pulse that raced at his throat. "I don't remember this part."

He settled his hands at her waist, coaxed with a caress. "What part don't you remember?"

His voice flowed over her like warmed wine. Inside, she felt liquid and light-headed, steeped in longing. "The part where you asked if you could kiss me."

He pressed his forehead to hers. "I was younger then. I took what I wanted."

Her breath, along with her better judgment, feathered out on a shivery sigh. "What do you want now, Garrett?"

A groan came from deep in his chest as he pulled her flush against him. "This. I want this."

What he wanted wasn't the chaste, tentative kiss of a schoolgirl. What he wanted was the rich, drugging kiss of a woman. She offered it to him. And he took it. Without hesitation. With hunger and need.

But still, she sensed his restraint. She could feel it in the tensile strength of the arms he wrapped around her. She could taste it in the way he covered her mouth with his and trembled with the wanting to ravage her.

She let herself go with it. Let herself feel the steel of his arms, the heat of his big body. And she reveled in the depth of his desire.

They were both breathless when he pulled away. Both poised on the edge of wanting to take the kiss to another level. And she might have let it happen if he hadn't set her away with unsteady hands and a grim resolve.

His eyes had darkened to midnight. "Good night, Em."

It was almost painful to see him that way. His control was a fluid thing—she sensed she could snap it with one word. One touch.

The jolt of power she felt in that moment was frightening and humbling—and empowering. She had to digest that. Assess it before she would know what to do with it.

"Good night, Garrett." Her voice, though a whisper, fractured the silence and the building tension.

"Sweet dreams." He trailed the back of his fingers across her cheek. "I'll see you in the morning."

"In the morning," she echoed, and watched him cross the room and slip outside into the night.

With quiet wonder she climbed the loft stairs. The small light by the bed cast the room in a muted glow as she undressed and slipped into her gown. The sheets were cool—as was the summer night in the mountains.

She lay awake and listened to its sounds. Always the

wind murmured through the trees. In the far distance a horned owl called, "Who...who...whooo?"

Below the loft, the back door opened, then closed with a low creak, signaling that Garrett had come back inside. The sound of bare feet on bare wood floors drifted upward. She heard a muted, shuffling sound, a click, a low whirring, then soft music playing.

With a catch in her breast, she recognized the sounds of him undressing: the rasp of a zipper going down; well-washed denim sliding down long, muscled legs. And she could picture him in the dark, plumping a pillow beneath his head, cool sheets rustling over his lean, hard body as he settled onto the sofa where he'd chosen to spend the night.

She turned to her side, curled into herself and tried not to think of his heat and his length and the fire he'd brought to a slow, burning flame with his good-night kiss.

"Who...who...whooo?" swooped into the darkness again, a lonesome, echoing reminder that she was still searching for who she was and where this was heading.

The bay mare had a soft mouth and solid footing. Garrett had selected her for both reasons from the small herd they still kept at the home place—and for her size and her temperament. Without any fuss she went wherever he asked her to go and easily handled the weight of him and Emma riding double.

He wasn't handling things quite as well. With Emma settled behind him, every shift of the big quarter horse's weight beneath them brought a bone-melting, blood boiling brush of her breasts against his back. Every change of direction, every descent downhill, had her slim thighs and hips cupping and hugging his like snug warm velvet.

It was hell. It was heaven. Being this close to her and not being able to do anything about it was slowly, systematically driving him crazy.

The horseback ride had seemed like such a good idea—a reenactment of their second date. After they'd showered and polished off a big breakfast this morning, he'd suggested the ride. She'd lit up like a shooting star.

He'd congratulated himself on his choice of activities. That was before he'd mounted up, pulled her up behind him and realized his error. They'd covered miles of ridges and rills since they'd started. And he wasn't in a congratulatory mood any longer.

They'd basked in the dappled sunlight filtering down through the trees, shared silent pleasure at the breathtaking beauty of the mountains and valley—while he'd died a thousand small deaths at every intimate encounter, at the hush of her breath at his nape, at her long, elegant fingers gripped at his waist.

He was as tense as a string on a crossbow. As edgy as the cliffs they'd climbed and descended.

In desperation he gauged the angle of the sun as they broke through the trees. "I'd say it's close to noon. How about we find a place to rest the horse and tie into that lunch we packed?" he suggested with a concerted effort to keep his tone light.

"Sounds good. I could use a little break myself. It's been a long time since I've spent this much time on horseback."

When she stretched and resettled her weight behind him to emphasize her agreement, he nearly bit a hole through the side of his cheek.

Looking around desperately, he spotted a site by the riverbank and kneed the mare into a fast jog.

"This'll do," he said without asking for her opinion, and reined in. The mare had barely skidded to a stop when he swung his leg over the pommel and bailed off.

Grim-faced, he turned back to her and lifted his hands to help her down. Though she looked at him with confusion, the natural, trusting way she leaned toward him and settled her hands on his shoulders was the catalyst he needed. It smoothed out the edges of tension and reminded him what this was all about.

It was about time. And trust. And slowly finding their way back to each other.

He let out a deep breath, gave her waist an affectionate squeeze and set her away.

"I'll loosen the cinch strap and take off her bridle. Why don't you set the table?" He handed her the pack that contained both a blanket and their lunch.

"Sounds like a plan." Arms full, she scanned the area for the perfect spot.

She selected well. He told her as much when he walked back to her side.

"How could I have missed? This entire valley—it's so...accessible," she said, finally deciding on the right word. "The Tetons are gorgeous, but except for all the public-park areas and the hordes of people who go with them, there's no single spot where you can be a part of both the beauty and the solitude. It's awesome."

So was she. The exercise, a good night's sleep, some rib-sticking food, and the color had begun to creep back into her cheeks. A gentle light had also replaced the dullness of lost hope in her eyes.

He'd like to think he was responsible for some of those slight, subtle changes. In truth, he knew the credit went to her. She'd always been a strong woman. In her soft, Southern way, she'd handled any obstacle that got in her path. It was only during the last few months before she'd left him that he'd sensed that strength ebbing. Then as now, he wondered at the cause.

Soon enough they'd tackle that issue. Right now it was enough to see her pulling herself together. That effort, in his estimation, was what strength was all about. Phoenix rising from the mythical ashes. The transformation was stunning. The promise worth waiting for.

"I can see why you and your brothers wanted to keep this to yourselves," she said as they spread the blanket for their table.

He was thoughtful for a moment. "The valley has always been magic for me. For the three of us boys playing outlaw and posse, it was a stage, a huge, wild amphitheater to play out our fantasies."

He paused for a moment, choosing his words carefully. "Even as we've grown older, it's been a source of memories and reflections—kind of like an old friend who was always here, waiting."

For a man fighting for his marriage, Garrett mused, it was also a courting ground to win back the woman he loved. As well-known turf, the advantage and the odds were in his favor here.

Yet even as he spoke, he knew he wasn't playing for advantage. He was speaking from his heart. And with all his heart he believed in the magic of love. "Now that you're here I know it's been waiting for you, too."

In a silence they both used to absorb the significance of his words, they settled on the blanket. Only then did Garrett take a moment to look—really look—around him.

"I know this spot," he said, a little taken aback that he hadn't recognized it right away.

"You know every spot in this valley." She handed him a sandwich and an apple.

"What I mean is, this was a special spot when we were kids. See that big boulder over there—the big brown one that looks kind of like a bottle lying on its side?"

She looked at the boulder, engaged her imagination and decided that yes, in a stretch, it could look like a bottle.

"If you look close enough you can make out where we scratched out our initials." He grinned at the memory. "We used to spend hours here searching for the gold."

Following her lead, he sat cross-legged beside her, doffed his Stetson and accepted the can of soda she'd dug out of the pack.

"Gold? What gold?"

"Frank and Jesse's."

She considered him over her sandwich. "Correct me if I'm wrong, but I thought Frank and Jesse James terrorized the good folks a little farther east and south of here—as in Arkansas and Missouri."

"Oh, they did. But you forget—they *are* my great, great uncles. And every family has secrets that it keeps."

He smiled, remembering how much stock he, Clay and Jesse had taken in the legend and lore. "Dad used to love to tell stories about them and how only the family knew about this place and the fact that they'd hidden out here because no one would expect them this far west.

"Supposedly they stashed a gold shipment—from a

train robbery in Arkansas—here in the valley. We spent a good part of each summer up here looking for it.''

"But you never found it.''

"Not a trace. We did find a few clues—an old gun handle, a rusted hinge that could have come from a lockbox. Some fired shell casings. Enough to keep us on the trail.''

"It must have been fun.''

He turned his head. Considered. "Yeah. Yeah, it was. It was fun looking. Fun believing.''

"And now? Do you still believe?''

He looked out over the river. It was shallow here, as it usually was in July, no more than knee-deep and as clear as the day was warm. As clear as the feelings he had for this woman.

"I never stopped believing. In a lot of things," he added, and allowed himself the luxury of looking deep into her eyes.

She believed, too. He could see it. She believed in them, and she'd decided she wasn't going to give up. Not yet. If things went the way he planned, not ever.

"It's been too long since I've come up here," he said, and heard the contemplative regret in his tone.

"You've missed it.''

"Yeah. I have.'' His sandwich gone, he eased back on his elbows, stretched out his legs and crossed his ankles in front of him on the blanket. In the enfolding warmth of the July sunshine, he watched the mare graze peacefully fifty yards away and thought not of serenity but of loss.

"You miss your father.''

Her quiet statement brought his head around. Her insight was frightening. And a little numbing. He'd been sixteen when his father died. It had been years after his death that he'd finally felt he had the strength—and the right—to come back to the valley. It had taken all the boys a long time to return—and they rarely came together. It was too hard. Alone it had been a little easier to make peace with the memories. And in his case, to struggle with the guilt.

"Do you want to talk about it?"

Her soft voice slipped into his thoughts like a gentle hand. Still, his body tensed.

"You miss him," she repeated. "Yet you've never talked about how losing him affected you. As a boy. As a man."

She was right. And it was probably a mistake to deny her access to those feelings. He did it, anyway. After all these years, they were still too difficult to share— even with her. Especially with her.

"It's too pretty a day to spend it sifting through dark memories." He smiled to take the edge off his rebuff.

Her face grew solemn, and he knew he had just put every inch of ground he'd gained at risk. But he couldn't. He couldn't open his own wounds and succeed in healing hers.

He touched a hand to her cheek. "I promise—some-day we'll talk about it. Just don't ask me to do it today. Today is too special. And I'm a man with a mission," he finished before she could voice a protest.

Emma wrestled with the weight of disappointment, but got sidetracked when he sat up and started tugging off his boots and socks.

"A mission?" she asked suspiciously. "What kind of mission?"

His smile was wicked and utterly irresistible. "One that involves water. We used to wade in this stretch of the river for hours—building dams, trying to catch trout with our hands.''

When he reached for her feet, she completely forgot about his evasive tactics and shifted into self-preservation mode. She scooted to the edge of the blanket, tucked her feet beneath her. ''What are you doing?''

''What? You forgot about my foot fetish?'' Laughing, he tugged her feet onto his lap.

She squirmed, gave in to a nervous laugh and fought valiantly to get away. He was too quick. And too strong. He made fast work of peeling off her shoes and socks.

''You don't have a foot fetish,'' she sputtered as he rose to his bare feet, hauled her up beside him then scooped her into his arms.

''I don't?'' Pretending to consider, he walked barefoot toward the riverbank. ''You know, I believe you're right. I must have been thinking of Jesse.''

''You were launching a diversion,'' she accused, then let go of a startled shriek when he hefted her higher.

With elaborate winces, clenched teeth and the occasional ''Ouch, dammit'' that had her smiling despite herself, he picked his way across the rocky river's edge and waded out into the water.

''Holy horse dung,'' he managed through huge, sharp breaths as the icy cold river washed over his ankles. ''It's freezing.''

''You are out of your mind.'' Charmed and taken with his antics and his efforts to make her smile, another burst of laughter sneaked out. ''And if you think for a minute I'm wading in that river of ice with you, you're beyond treatment.''

''It's invigorating,'' he managed between careful steps as he splashed deeper into the current.

"I can see that," she agreed, clinging to his neck like a lifeline. "It's invigorating the heck out of your teeth. You're going to chip a tooth with all that chattering."

"You'll love it," he assured her, refusing to be swayed.

"You can love it for me. I'm not going in."

"What? No spirit of adventure?" His eyes danced with a hint of challenge.

"No wish for pneumonia."

"It's only a shock for a little while," he insisted. "I hardly notice the cold now."

"That's probably because your feet are numb. Does the term *hypothermia* strike any chords?"

His grin developed into a full fledged dare. "If I didn't know better, I'd say you were chicken."

Instead of denying it, she clucked loud and long, then screamed lustily when he let his arm slip out from under her legs and her toes skimmed the top of the water.

As nimble as Sara, she tightened her hold around his neck, wrapped her legs around his waist and locked her ankles.

Surprised by the quickness of her countermove, his hands moved instinctively to her bottom to steady her.

"This is getting interesting." The glint in his eyes hinted at the focus of that interest.

She felt the blush all the way to her bare toes. "I repeat—I'm not going in."

He cocked his head, still grinning. "Tell you what. I'll trade you one thrilling experience for another."

She loosened her grip on his neck long enough to brush the hair out of her eyes. "Now we're playing 'Let's Make a Deal'?"

"Now we're just playing." His beautiful features had

relaxed. His tone was intimate and rich with memories. "Like we used to. Remember?"

Oh, yes. She remembered. They used to play and tease and just plain have fun. Until last night she'd almost forgotten what it was like. She hadn't let herself acknowledge how much she'd missed this foolishness, this childlike nonsense. Just like she hadn't let herself admit how much she'd missed his kisses.

"I remember," she whispered as his gaze lowered to her mouth and his hands swept the length of her back in long, lazy strokes.

"I'm going to kiss you, Em." His voice was gruff with intent when he lowered his mouth to hers. "I thought you'd like to know that—but this time, I'm not going to ask for permission."

Seven

His kiss was warm and tender. Her response was electric and hot. It took her by surprise. Took them both by storm. Fueled by the sunshine, hastened by the summer breeze, tentative and sweet became in a heartbeat demanding and dark…and she dragged him along for the ride.

Need, full and pulsing, rushed through her blood with the recklessness of the river. It flowed wildly, ran rampant. Clinging to him, she knotted her fingers in his hair, tightened her legs around his waist.

With a groan of surprise and pleasure, he deepened the kiss, tasted her with his tongue when she tempted him, then welcomed him inside.

His hands were suddenly everywhere. His breath slogged out, ragged and rushed. He crushed his arms around her, spread his legs wide for balance—then stumbled on the rocky riverbed when she squirmed, shifting her weight to get closer.

And then they were falling. No amount of scrambling footwork, no abundance of his physical strength could stop the inevitable pull of gravity.

He twisted at the last second to take the brunt of the fall. Fast, furious and explosive, they hit the water with a thrashing splash.

The cold blast doused the heat of their kiss like a bucket of ice. They landed with her on top of him. Though a foot and a half of water cushioned their fall, the shock was still bruising. She rolled off him with the speed of a rocket and landed on her butt beside him.

Spitting water, she gasped for air that the fall and the brittle cold had stolen. When she could take a breath that didn't feel like it was her last, she dragged wet hair from her face—then felt her heart skid into a rare panic. Garrett lay flat on his back, as still as death.

She scrambled frantically to stand. Planting her feet on either side of his hips, she grabbed fistfuls of his shirt and pulled. He reared up so quickly she lost her balance and landed on his lap, straddling him, while he laughed like a loon. Laughed, damn him, when she'd been afraid he was hurt—or worse.

Temper shot through fear like a bullet. "This is not funny!"

He threw back his head and roared, his shoulders heaving with laughter.

Royally miffed now, she rapped him a good one in the chest. She got fresh gales for her efforts as he wiped a hand over his wet face.

"You fool. I thought you were hurt."

His eyes sparkled, those beautiful pearly whites gleamed whiter in the sunlight. "Oh, I am. I definitely am. I'm betting there's a bruise the size of Texas on my left cheek.''

She didn't want to respond to that grin of his that not only lit his face with mirth but did its best to coax a smile out of her.

''Are you okay?'' he managed around a chuckle.

''Yes,'' she admitted with a sniff to let him know she was still angry, even as the insistent twitch of her lips curved into an answering grin. ''I'm fine. If you don't count the fact that I'm freezing to death.''

An involuntary shiver reinforced her statement.

''You've got goose bumps.'' Suddenly contrite, he rubbed her arms with the flat of his hands to warm her.

More than her arms warmed up. And her skin wasn't the only part of her body that reacted involuntarily to the cold—and to his touch. She became aware of another, more interesting, change the same time he did.

The laughter in his eyes had faded. In its place a melting warmth intensified to a burn.

Slowly she followed the track of his gaze.

Beneath lacy bra cups and the light cotton of her white T-shirt, her nipples had tightened into hard peaks. They pressed provocatively against the wet fabric, stiff from the cold and a sudden spike of arousal.

''I suppose,'' he said, his voice gone deep and heavy with the weight of arousal, ''we'd better get you out of here before you catch that cold you were trying to avoid.''

''Yes,'' she echoed softly as the sensitivity of her breasts became almost unbearable and the intimate press of their bodies where she straddled his lap made her ache. ''I suppose we'd better.''

Only she didn't move. She couldn't. Not with him watching her that way. Not when she wanted him to touch her, to taste her through wet cotton and steal the last of the chill from her blood.

"Em?"

The huskiness of his murmur shivered up her spine like rough, restless fingertips. Watching his mouth, remembering how he tasted, how he wanted, she slowly licked a drop of water from her upper lip.

Garrett groaned. She had no idea. She hadn't a single clue how she was affecting him. She couldn't have or she'd have been running for her life.

She was a siren in wet denim and clinging cotton. Her breasts were round and full. The dark center of her nipples pebbled into tight erotic peaks. He knew what they felt like between his fingertips, how to change velvet to diamonds with his touch. He knew how she tasted, like sweetness and sensation and sex.

And he knew he had to put some distance between them, or he'd answer the invitation in her heavy-lidded eyes and start something she wasn't ready to finish.

With all the will he possessed he clamped his hands around her waist. Jaw set in determination, he lifted her up and off him, letting go only when he was sure she was on solid footing.

Only then did he dare stand up, thankful the icy water had put a damper on his physical reaction to the sensual picture she made standing there.

"We'd better head back," he said gruffly.

He saw her confusion, gave her the moment she needed for reality to grip her and to recognize that he was backing off. A moment more to remember why.

With a quick, embarrassed smile, she averted her gaze to the river and its scrambling dance over rock and stone.

She worked hard to collect herself. For several seconds her face was fierce with concentration—a concentration that shifted abruptly. Self-conscious awareness gave way to intense curiosity as her brows knit together and she honed in on a spot several yards away.

Before he could ask what she was thinking, she splashed away from him toward a wide spot in the river.

"Em—" he plowed his fingers through his wet hair "—what are you—"

"Wait…wait a second." She held up a hand, cutting him off.

Knee-deep in water, she bent over and stuck her arm in up to her elbow. She fished around, then dug in with both hands to tug aside a rock. When she straightened, she was clutching a shiny round disk the size of a silver dollar in her hand.

"Garrett—look at this."

He waded over beside her.

"Is it—could it possibly be?" The brightness in her eyes was out-brillianced only by the glint of sunshine bouncing off the water—and by the glitter of the coin pinched between her fingers.

She offered it to him, anticipation lighting her eyes and coloring her cheeks. He turned it over, tested its weight in his palm, studied it carefully.

"It's gold," he said at last.

"I knew it!" She fairly bubbled with excitement. "Frank and Jesse's?"

He scratched his jaw, took a closer look. "It looks old enough."

He handed the gold piece back to her with a smile that essentially translated to pride. "You did it, Em. You did what none of us James boys had been able to do. You found the treasure—at least a part of it. It's the first real proof that it actually might exist. I'd suggest you tuck this someplace where it won't get away from you."

Warmed by his smile, she buried the gold piece in her pocket and humming with excitement, scanned the riverbed through the crystal clear water. "Maybe there's more."

His slow nod confirmed that he'd been thinking the same thing.

As exuberant as children, they searched for another half hour, but gave up on finding any more coins when the cold water forced them to the shore.

They collapsed on the blanket to let the rays of the sun warm them and finish drying their clothes.

Emma slipped the coin out of her pocket, amazed at its golden color, fascinated by the body heat it had captured and retained even as she held it.

"It's beautiful, isn't it?" she murmured, pleasantly exhausted, but riding on the wonder of her find.

"*You're* beautiful."

The gruffness of his voice stilled the absent caress of her fingers over the coin's shining surface. She was far from beautiful—her clothes were damp and clingy, her hair was windblown and straggly from the water and she wasn't wearing a drop of makeup—yet the look in his eyes, when she met them, made her feel as beautiful as he wanted her to be.

Something changed between them in that moment. Something she couldn't positively identify or definitively name. While it was less than a resolution, it felt like much more than a beginning.

What it was, she decided after a moment, was a comfortable common ground, a similar path, and she liked the direction it was taking. Had liked it since they'd shared the wonder of a kiss last night on the steps to the loft. Had wanted it since their heated kiss in the swirling waters of the icy river had renewed an ache both painful and sweet.

Something changed inside her, too. A new confidence, born of his desire for her, added perspective and strengthened her sense of self. Deciding that, like the river, she would go with the flow and see where it took them, she smiled into his velvet blue eyes. "You just want my gold."

He cocked his head, then touched her with a smile so soft and tender she felt caressed. "There is that."

They shared a quick grin.

"But you are beautiful. I like seeing you smile, Em. It makes me wish I could find you a bucket of gold."

It's not the gold, she wanted to tell him. It was the moment that was golden, it was the man who had made it so. But she couldn't say it. Not yet. Ultimately not ever, if they didn't cross that invisible line and open up to each other. If she didn't cross the line herself and open up to him.

Her newfound confidence helped her fight off old feelings—far too familiar feelings—of inadequacy and isolation. Even though they tried to inch into the warmth of the July afternoon and undercut the memories they were beginning to make, she wouldn't let them.

They were getting close. When she'd asked him earlier about his father, they'd been so close to bridging what she felt was a huge gap between them. If he would break down and talk to her about something so personal, so painful, she knew she would have had the strength to do the same.

Yes, he'd closed himself off from her today—like he

always closed himself off when he had a problem, not realizing that in turn it made her feel the need to conceal her problems from him.

That had been one of their biggest sources of miscommunication. But that was going to change. She knew he'd give her anything—his wealth, his protection, his desire—anything but the part of him he felt he needed to keep under lock and key. And it was that part of him—the knowledge of what made him weak, the key to what made him strong—that she needed most if they were going to put their life back together.

Three months ago those same feelings of inadequacy she'd successfully wrestled aside today had driven her to the edge. She knew that now. Just as she knew he would never cheat on her. But her strength had been weakened then, her sense of self diminished. She just hadn't been able to see it.

She wasn't going to get caught up in that defeated mind-set again, she decided, as she sat there under the baking warmth of the sun and the question in his eyes. Not now that they'd gotten this far. Garrett was right about so many things. She wasn't her mother; he wasn't her father. And the past they had together was a good one. No longer was she willing to let their future slip away without a fight.

Strengthened by that conviction, empowered by that newfound strength and by the feelings she had for this man, she ran her thumb over the shining warmth of the coin.

With a new determination and renewed hope, she tossed it in the air. Sunlight caught its sheen, fired the gold as it arched, flipping end over end.

Garrett snagged it out of the air on the fly. He studied

it, studied her. "A little careless with your treasure, aren't you?"

She had been careless, Emma acknowledged, as eyes as crystalline and clear as the sky penetrated hers. They'd both been careless with something far more precious than gold. They'd been careless with each other. That was going to have to end if they were ever going to find their way back to what they'd once had. She decided right then and there that she'd do everything in her power to make that happen.

"Never," she said, holding his gaze. "Never again."

She folded her fingers around his until the coin was swallowed by the loose fist of his hand. "Why don't you hang on to it for me. Hang on until I tell you to let go."

The sun was a burning ball of apricot gold and blushing rose when they rode back to the cabin. Garrett offered Emma first shot at the shower while he bedded down the mare and fed her.

He needed a little time away from her to settle himself down. He needed some time to think.

Still revved from the events of the afternoon, he couldn't shake the picture of her, golden and glowing. Couldn't dull the feel of her against him, warm and wet and willing. And more, he couldn't deny the notion that there had been a subtle shift in the way she reacted to him. There had been a definitive softness in her eyes. A deeper meaning in her words.

They were closing the gap. Every instinct he trusted told him so. Just like they told him that now, more than ever, he needed to tread carefully. He couldn't blow this. And he would if he didn't figure out a way to rein in his libido.

That was the hard part—literally, he conceded with a grim set of his lips—and he didn't know how much longer he could keep it in check. Not long if she kept responding to him the way she had last night and again this afternoon.

So he deliberately took his time with the mare. He even took the time to gather wood for a fire he doubted they would need, even though the promise of a night chill had drifted in on the late-afternoon air.

He stared at the cabin long and hard before he climbed the porch steps and dumped the armload of split ash into the wood box by the door. Satisfied he was ready to handle another celibate night, he drew a deep breath and ducked into the cabin.

Emma was nowhere to be seen, but the soft creak of the wood floor overhead told him she was up in the loft. Grateful for another few minutes to pull it all together, he headed straight for the shower—and felt his resolve slip a notch then spiral out of orbit and into free fall.

The small bathroom was still steeped in the residual fragrance of her shower. Like her lingerie, Maya had picked out her shampoo. The scent was subtly floral, provocatively feminine. Undeniably sensual. Images—old and new—of him and Emma sharing steam and soap and sex under the warm fingers of a shower spray had him stripping off his shirt and jeans and cooling himself down with ice water for the second time that day.

His blood and his body were chilled to the point of frosting over when he finally cranked off the taps. Whipping wet hair from his face, he stuck his hand past the shower curtain and reached for a towel. When he came up empty, he shoved aside the curtain—then felt his heart hit a solid ten on the Richter scale.

Emma was standing there, the towel in her hand.

"Is this what you're looking for?"

Her voice was whisper soft, Southern seductive, as void of innocence or pretense as the smoky invitation in her eyes.

His heart actually stopped then. He felt it. The heavy thud. The electric stall. The agonizing stillness before it picked up the beat, hard, heavy and harried.

"Thanks," he said when he could find his voice. Eyes on her, he took the towel from her extended hand. She leaned back against the sink, boldly watched as he dragged it over his body.

Her hair hung damp and shining over her shoulder, the belt of her rose silk robe was looped loosely at her waist. Her dark eyes assessing him, she shifted, then braced her hands on the counter beside her hips when he knotted the towel low at his waist. The rose-colored lapels gaped open. The sight of the long, sleek length of her bare leg, the pale curve of a breast, barely covered by the black French lace of a skimpy teddy, made a joke of the restraint he'd prided himself on possessing.

He'd wanted desperately to keep things slow and sweet and comfortable. But she'd just shrunk the comfort zone to the size of a postage stamp. And slow and sweet had become the impossible dream.

He read the slumberous look in her eyes for the invitation it was and knew that right or wrong, he was going to accept it.

He stepped out of the shower. Stepped against her and felt all his blood pool in his loins where their bodies connected.

"I had this all planned," he said gruffly. "It was going to be slow." He lowered his mouth to her throat, tugged at the belt of her robe when she arched her neck in invitation.

"I was going to romance you." Her instant, shivering response stole his breath as he shoved rose silk from her shoulders and let it fall at her feet on the floor. "With flowers," he growled between a string of open-mouthed, biting kisses that tracked the length of her jawline, "and candlelight."

When she sighed, a throaty, pleasured sound, he scooped her into his arms and headed for the loft. "And music. There was going to be music, dammit."

He felt her smile against his lips as she curled her arms around his neck. "I'm sorry to spoil your plans."

He groaned when she opened her mouth and dragged him into a kiss so deep, so drugging, he had to stop midway up the stairs to taste and plunder and claim.

His towel drifted to the floor as he lowered her to the bed. "I'll deal with it." He nuzzled the fragrant hollow between her breasts and tugged the scrap of sexy black lace from her shoulder. "I'll improvise."

And then he lost himself in the wonder of her. In the delicate fullness of her breasts, the satin of her belly, the creamy resilience of her thighs.

Seeing her like this, half-naked, wholly needy for him, was an erotic homecoming, months of midnight dreams.

"Look at me." His hand trembled as he skimmed it over a bared breast. "I'm shaking like it was the first time."

"It feels like the first time." Breathless, she covered his hand with hers and guided it to her other breast. "You steal my breath."

And she stole his heart—just like she had the first time he'd seen her smile. The first time he'd dared to kiss her, the first touch of his calloused hand on the sensitive tip of her nipple.

Her willingness, the unexpected offering of her body, finally did what all of his self-discipline hadn't been able to accomplish. With aching restraint, he reined in his desire.

This was the woman he loved. This was the woman he had almost lost. He wasn't going to take the chance of losing her again—not in a wild, primitive rush to satisfy his own suddenly insatiable needs.

He raised his head, brushed the hair from her face. Smiled into her passion-glazed eyes.

"Make love to me, Garrett." She arched to him, restless and needy when he shifted his weight to her side.

"I am, sweet Emma. I am."

With a gentleness reserved just for her, he eased the lace teddy down her hips and tossed it aside. With a patience that spoke of his love, he tended to the flesh he revealed.

With his hands and his mouth he petted and stroked and brought her to an edge cut sharp with the sting of pleasure, tempered with the urgency of need.

"Easy," he whispered, when he cupped her intimately and she cried his name. "Just go with it."

She groaned low and deep and rocked straining hips into the caress of his fingers. "I need you. Inside me. I need you...with me."

"Soon." He lowered his head to pinch a taut nipple between his teeth and suckled. "Soon," he promised, drugged by the taste of her on his tongue, by the heat and wetness of her sliding against his fingers. "This time is for you—just for you."

With a tortured moan, she stiffened, shuddered and poured into his hand.

Her total absorption in sensation was the most erotic sight he'd ever seen. Knowing that it was to him and him alone she gave herself was more satisfying than his own release—and gave him the strength to stall it.

He gathered her close as her trembling eased and she turned limp and languid in his arms. "My God, you're beautiful."

Emma couldn't talk. Could barely breathe, and at the moment didn't care if she ever had a cognizant thought again, other than the one attached to the pleasure he'd just given her.

It had been so long. So long since he'd touched her like this. So long since she'd felt she could let him. Even before she'd left him, they'd pulled away from each other physically as well as emotionally.

She shifted in his arms. Lifted heavy eyes to his. He trailed a finger down her cheek. She caught it in her hand, drew it to her mouth. It tasted of him, of her, and it sparked a renewed spike of desire so hot she felt singed by the flame.

"Now," she demanded, as she drew him on top of her and opened her body to take him in.

"Now," he ground out as he filled her with his length and claimed her. "Now and forever."

He entered and withdrew in thick, silken thrusts and deep, driving glides. She locked her legs around his waist, dug her fingers into his shoulders and rode to the crest of each towering swell. He stroked her to yet another orgasm, this one so stunning, so endless, she lost time, lost presence, lost awareness of everything but his thrilling heat and carnal rhythms.

He filled her completely, velvet steel to liquid silk, and with his own guttural groan of release, shot over the peak and into the abyss of dark, drenching pleasure.

Garrett knew the moment she came awake. Had loved watching the gentle transition from deep sleep to dreamy consciousness.

He stroked his hand over a pale, slim hip, kneading softly. Lowering his mouth to the velvet tip of her breast, he nuzzled, lavishly laved. Her response was so perfect, so purely and wantonly selfish, he smiled against her breast and drew her deeper.

A limp hand fell to his hair, caressed him, pressed him closer in abandoned invitation to taste and sample more.

"I've missed this. Missed waking up to you like this," he whispered, shifting his attention to her other breast. "Sated, sleepy, completely submissive."

She purred. It could only be called a purr as she shivered, and in a fluid, graceful move, turned the tables on him. Pressing him to his back, she pinned his shoulders to the mattress with her hands. Watching his face, she leaned into him, brushing her breasts across his chest. "We'll see about submissive."

She drove him out of his mind—at least she tried to. As always, with Emma, he took care to keep himself in check. She'd been barely eighteen the first time they'd made love. She'd been a virgin. He'd been more experienced than he'd had a right to be—and wrong to take advantage. It hadn't stopped him from wanting her. Hadn't stopped him from loving her. But it had made him mindful enough to take great care.

He'd been taking care ever since. His need for her was so huge, so consuming, he was afraid if he ever let himself go completely, he'd destroy her—physically and emotionally.

He took care now. Care to keep his need confined. Care to give more than he took. Care to see to her needs before his.

She fought the descent from aggressor to supplicant. Battled the transition of power. His assault was relentless and artful. For each move she made, he countered, feeding her flame, building her desire until her focus shifted. Until her yearning to please him became a restless demand to be pleased.

With lush strokes and smoky kisses he coaxed her over that edge again where her body clenched, her breath caught, and she begged him to tumble her over the peak.

Loving her, loving the feel of her, the need in her, he followed, his own demise mellow and blissfully sweet.

His growling stomach and a definite chill roused him a couple of hours later. Careful not to wake her, Garrett eased out of bed, pulled on jeans and a shirt and crept quietly down the stairs.

After pouring himself a huge glass of milk, he hunted up the beef stew Maya had made up and sent with him. He'd just finished his first bowl when Emma tiptoed down the stairs and joined him in the kitchen.

Her face was sleep flushed, her hair beautifully and provocatively mussed. She dragged her fingers through it, her expression sober as she wrapped the rose silk robe tighter around her.

He went to her, drew her into his arms, held her for a moment.

"You okay?"

"I'm fine."

She pulled slowly away, busied herself finding a bowl and a spoon.

Everything in her response—from the stiff set of her

shoulders, to her unwillingness to face him—suggested otherwise.

"Em?" He caught her arm. Turned her toward him. "Sweetheart—what is it? What's wrong?"

"Nothing's wrong," she insisted, closed her eyes, then opened them with a forced smile in place. "I'm just…just a little nervous about this, I guess."

"Nervous?" It took a moment of confusion before it finally came to him. When it did, his conscience kicked into overdrive.

"It was too soon, wasn't it? I knew I was rushing you."

"No. It wasn't too soon. And you didn't rush me." Banked impatience clipped her words. She checked it and made another game attempt at a smile. "I came to you, remember?"

He did remember. That's why she was confusing the hell out of him. "Then what? What is it?" The cause came to him like a sledge dropped on his chest. "Em…was I too rough with you?"

Her smile was too quick. Her laugh a little too brittle. "No, Garrett. You weren't rough. You're never rough. You were the perfect gentleman. You took good care of me."

Somehow she had managed to make that sound distasteful. Before he could question her on it, she flashed him another one of those overbright smiles. "Just…give me a little time to adjust to…to us. To this physical part of us again, okay?"

Again she smiled. And still, he felt there was more she wasn't telling him.

"Now, were you going to feed me, or am I going to have to stand here with my empty bowl like Oliver Twist all night?"

With a frown creasing his brow, he took the bowl she extended and filled it with stew. When he joined her at the table, whatever he'd sensed—or thought he'd sensed—was wrong, was no longer there. In its place was a bubbling enthusiasm at the prospect of returning to the spot where she'd found the gold piece to continue the search the next day.

Through it all, though, an unnamed concern niggled in the back of his mind. Yet when she led him back to the loft and let him make love to her again under the downy warmth of the bed covers, he let the night and the moment and the woman take him—and forgot that everything wasn't exactly right with his world.

Eight

The next time Emma awoke it was to daylight and a silence broken only by the deep even breaths of the man sleeping by her side. Garrett had wrapped himself around her like a warm, heavy blanket. She felt treasured and protected—yet weighted with a niggling concern that wouldn't let her take comfort in the haven he offered.

Not wanting to wake him, but needing some thinking room, she eased carefully from the cocoon of his arms. Wrapped in her robe, she tiptoed down the loft stairs and made a pot of coffee. With a steaming mug in her hand, she snagged a blanket from the sofa and slipped outside. Then she settled herself in the big willow chair on the porch to decide where to go from here.

The morning sparkled. Birdsong drifted on the air like a concerto. Sunlight caught the restlessly shifting waters of the river. It glittered like an unraveling bolt of diamond-studded silk.

The beauty was stunning—yet all she could see was the magnitude of the problems they still faced.

Making love with Garrett may have eased the sexual tension that had been building like a summer storm; it may have been beautiful and breached the barrier of physical intimacy, but it hadn't really solved any of their deep-seated problems.

Last night, in bed, Garrett had unintentionally shown her just how many issues they still had to resolve if they were going to get their marriage back on track.

But how could she tell him that? How could she explain to him that his lovemaking had been sweet and sexy and totally solicitous to her needs, and then make him understand that it wasn't enough? How could she explain that it had been wonderful and that he'd given her everything she could possibly want? Everything but himself and the latitude to share the control in their lovemaking and in their lives? How could she make him understand that his inability to let himself be totally free with her in bed carried over to other areas of their relationship and was at the root of the problem that had led them to this point?

She hugged the warm mug with both hands, let out a deep breath. Garrett was a very prideful man. He was a man who shouldered responsibility—no matter how great—without complaint. He didn't have a selfish urge inside him, yet his inability to share the reins of responsibility in their relationship made her feel like she was being denied something vital. Something that would allow her to be a partner instead of someone who needed to be provided for.

But Garrett was a man who couldn't, in his wildest

dreams, imagine asking the woman he loved to share the load with him. Just like his sense of duty, he'd kept his problems to himself. The end result was that he shut her out of the important parts of his life. The parts that she could help with, if he would but let her. The parts that she could be for him what he always was for her—essential.

For years she'd tried not to feel diminished by the way he held everything inside and by the restraint he imposed on his own needs.

And for all those years, she'd been wrong.

Closing her eyes, she let her head rest on the back of the chair and accepted the severity of that error. It made her as culpable in the disintegration of their relationship as he—more so, because she'd recognized what his inability to treat her as an equal was doing to her and she hadn't told him.

She'd always known she'd needed him to give her more credit for her own strengths. Yet last night when they'd made love, she'd let herself be manipulated into complacency again. She'd let him change the tempo, let his gentle ways and lavish loving take the power from her and reclaim it as his. And last night, as in the past ten years, she'd hurt them both by giving in so easily.

If they were going to fix what was wrong between them, she couldn't continue to let that happen. It was the easy way out. The coward's way. She couldn't continue to let him control the tone of their lovemaking—just like he controlled the tone of their lives—no matter how noble his motive.

Still, the question remained as she sipped her coffee and stared out over the valley: how did she make him understand without ripping to shreds the delicate threads of the fabric they'd begun to weave back together?

When the screen door opened half an hour later and Garrett stepped outside, she was still wrestling with the weight of a solution even as her heart melted at the look of him.

His hair was bed rumpled and beautifully mussed. He'd taken the time to tug on his jeans but nothing else. His feet were bare as he eased a hip on the porch rail and crossed his arms over his chest to stall a shiver. Goose bumps raced along his skin even as a warming sun struggled to steal the chill from the air.

"G'morning."

His voice was gruff with sleep, his eyes soft and indulgent.

He would never appreciate the thought, but at that moment this big, strong man who saw to everyone's needs but his own, looked as vulnerable as their daughter—and the last thing she wanted to do was hurt him. Not again. She'd done enough of that already.

"You'll catch your death," she scolded as he smiled into her eyes.

"Then I'd die a happy man."

Shoving away from the rail, he leaned slowly toward her, planted his hands on the chair's arms and covered her mouth with his.

His kiss was a gentle hello, the morning stubble of his beard pleasantly abrasive.

He pulled away, touched a finger to her cheek. "I'll go fix breakfast."

In silence she watched him go. In silence she told herself she had to be the one to initiate the fix. Then she prayed for the insight and the backbone to see it through.

She'd made up her mind to confront him over breakfast, yet when he came for her, fed her, then coaxed her back to the loft, she couldn't make herself do it. Not yet. Not with him looking at her that way, not with this renewed intimacy between them so delicate. Instead, she let him take her back to the loft and make love to her as if she were as fragile as glass.

As Garrett saddled the mare after breakfast then led her to the cabin to collect Emma, he told himself that everything was going great between them. She'd been open and giving and deliciously responsive in bed. There had been that moment last night in the kitchen, yes, but he'd since decided he'd just been looking for problems where none existed. Her explanation—a slight case of nerves—made sense. Hell, he'd been a little uptight himself.

And if she seemed a little distant this morning, well, it stood to reason that she might still be feeling vulnerable. She'd been emotionally exhausted when he'd brought her here. In just a couple of days, however, he'd seen a remarkable change. He'd been afraid for her when he'd stolen her away in the middle of the night. But she was evolving back to the Emma he'd fallen in love with, loving, laughing, giving. And he saw nothing but good for their future together.

Yet when she swung up behind him and they headed back toward the spot where she'd found her gold, every instinct he trusted told him something wasn't quite right, that he was only kidding himself if he thought otherwise.

The day was too perfect he decided, the mood too mellow to let unfounded suspicions dampen it. So he didn't let it. Together they searched for the gold in earnest. Together they smiled and laughed—and pretended that everything was exactly the way it should be between them.

When their search yielded nothing but cold feet and wet jeans, he led her back to the riverbank and laid her down on the blanket—then he loved her again by sunlight.

That evening he made good on the plans that had gone awry the night before. They dined by candlelight and soft music—music he'd selected especially to stir memories and enhance the mood.

Just like he'd found her favorite movie, he'd dug up songs from the year she'd graduated, songs from her senior prom. With a lovers' moon peeking through the window, casting a golden glow on her hair, they danced close in each other's arms, surrounded by memories and magic—then spent the night making love until any undercurrents of trouble were obliterated by exhaustion.

The next few days were filled with sunny mornings and steamy nights. They weren't any closer to finding the gold than they were when Emma had stumbled onto that single coin. But treasure, Emma decided, came in other forms that were equally as rich. She'd never been more confident of her love for this man. Never more confident of his love for her—yet never less certain of how to ensure that their love didn't get lost again in a maze of misunderstanding.

She'd had no luck getting Garrett to open up to her, but she had found a number of answers to her own questions up here in the mountains. Of most significance, she'd found herself again. She'd regained her emotional equilibrium. She wasn't teetering on that edge anymore.

She'd looked her weakness in the eye and faced it

down. Without Garrett it would have been hard, but she knew now that she could have done it. She also knew that she was glad she hadn't had to accomplish it without him.

By the afternoon of the fourth day, however, as she sat on the porch steps and watched Garrett working down by the river, she admitted that she'd been stalling. While she'd worried the problem in her mind over the past several days, even made token attempts to lead him to the brink of a confidence, or to completely letting go in bed, she'd repeatedly allowed him to skillfully and playfully manipulate the control away from her.

As she watched him fussing with the cabin's waterline, her heart swelled with love, yet felt crowded with fear for their future. Their week was almost up. In a couple of days they'd head back to Jackson—and she still hadn't forced the issue that would make or break their marriage.

It was then, as the fear made itself known with a vengeance, that she finally accepted the challenge. He wasn't going to cross that particular bridge with gentle prodding. Not when he still thought he was protecting her from himself—both physically and emotionally. Not when protecting her was Garrett's main mission in life.

It had never been in her nature to be confrontational, but time was running out. If she was going to be the woman he needed her to be, she had to force him to open up to her. And if they were going to leave Wind River and become a family again, she had to buck nature and anything else that got in her way.

Tonight, she decided, as he lifted his head and sent her a smile as warm as sunlight, was the night that would seal or sink their future together.

* * *

The evening temperature was balmy by Wind River standards. What breeze stirred, did so with the warm breath of summer as it sifted through the forest and perfumed the air with the scent of evergreen.

A heavenful of stars accompanied a full, rising moon, embellishing its golden light. The sound of a bluesy sax and lusty lyrics drifted from the CD player as Garrett led Emma out onto the porch and into the moonlight.

He folded her in his arms, kissed her and felt a completeness that three months ago he'd thought he'd lost forever. Everything he'd hoped for, everything he'd counted on happening here had played out exactly the way he'd planned it.

She was his again. She was Emma again. And nothing was ever going to come between them. After everything they'd been through, he'd make damn sure of it.

Bursting with the confidence that their marriage was safe, he drew her hand to his chest where his heart thrummed with excitement and anticipation. "Feel that? You do that to me, Em. Always."

Swaying with her in his arms, he moved to the music as it blended with the night sounds and the heavy rhythm of his heart.

"I remember this." She nestled her cheek on his shoulder. "It was the last song of the night at my senior prom."

"And the first night for something special for us."

"It was the first time we made love," she murmured.

He chuckled softly. "You don't know the agony I went through waiting for you…waiting for that night." He squeezed her hard. "So what do you think? Any chance of this night playing out like that one?"

He'd expected a coy smile. Instead a wistful sadness

darkened her eyes, and when she spoke, her voice sounded breathtakingly sad.

"It seems like it was so long ago. We were so young then. So in love and ignorant of the things that can go bad between a woman and a man."

Slowly she pulled away from him. Her fingers trailed out of his hand as she walked to the porch rail and gazed at the star-spackled sky above them.

Puzzled by her sudden melancholy, he walked up behind her, tugged her back against his chest and waited to hear what was on her mind.

"It was the most beautiful night of my life." She turned abruptly, searched his face with a sudden, surging expectancy. "I want to feel it again. That freedom. That shift from feeling weighted to weightless. Make me remember, Garrett. Make me remember what it felt like to live for the moment and love without care. Make me feel invincible again."

There was an urgency in her voice as she clung to him. A wildness in her eyes as she pulled his head to hers.

She asked for innocence—then enticed him with everything but. Capturing his mouth with hers, she lured him into a kiss that was demanding and hungry and tempered with a fierce desperation.

Her aggression shot him from surprised to fully aroused in one hot, fluid heartbeat. Desire spiked through his blood like a fever. He tried to check it but she dragged him under again. Her fingers knotted in his hair were brutal, her mouth devouring.

"Em...baby...slow down." His breath pumped out, harsh and heavy with the pulsing surge of passion.

She went on as if she hadn't heard him. Possessing him with her tongue and the erotic press of her breasts to his chest, she tore at his shirt, peeled it over his shoulders and yanked it down his arms.

"Sweet Je—" He groaned as she strung hungry, biting kisses along his jaw. He sucked in a harsh breath when she scraped her teeth over his nipple and, fighting his attempt to still her hands, went to work on his belt buckle.

Need, pure, primitive and carnal, snared him in its grasp when her long, elegant fingers opened his fly, stole inside and surrounded him.

Desire, consuming and suddenly insatiable, possessed him. He was past thinking as he fumbled frantically with the zipper on her jeans, then ripped them down her hips. Lust was a drug, a renegade craving that invaded his blood and set the animal inside him free.

He lifted her, pinned her against the outside wall of the cabin. Through a mind-numbing fog he felt the scrape of her fingernails on his back, was oblivious to the bruising possession of his hands on her hips.

It was her cry that stopped him from slamming himself into her. The fragility of her skin that arrested his hands.

With a smothered oath, he pushed away from her, cursing himself as he struggled with control and a guilt that bludgeoned him like a club.

He didn't know how much time passed until he felt he could touch her without taking her. Didn't know how long she leaned against the cabin for support, her eyes glazed with what could only be horror.

"Em." He caught her against him as much to steady her as to avoid dealing with the beaten look on her face. Shame, thick and cloying, swamped him. "I don't know where that came from. Baby, did I hurt you?"

"No." Her breath slogged out on short, labored puffs. "No, you didn't hurt me."

"I'm sorry. Christ. I'm so sorry."

She jerked away from his hold, her eyes dark and dangerously combatant. "I don't want you to be sorry."

Guilt crowded him. With a gentle hand he brushed the hair from her eyes. "I was rough with you. I practically mauled you."

She batted his hand away. "You were *real* with me. You took me. Or you were going to before that damnable honor of yours got in the way." Sparks shot from her eyes. "For once...for the first time...you almost let go of that control you take such pride in owning and took me like a woman."

Looking battered but somehow victorious, she reached for her jeans, dragged them on. "Don't take that away from me with apologies. For godsake, don't be sorry for that."

Shouldering away from him, she jerked open the cabin door and marched inside.

He stood in baffled silence and watched her go. He'd expected her anger. He deserved it. And she was mad as hell, all right—but not because he'd been rough, but because he'd apologized for it.

At a complete loss to understand what was happening, he scrubbed both hands over his face, then followed her into the cabin.

The music drifting from the CD player should have been soothing. Instead its mellow sound, so at odds with the turmoil he was feeling, was as annoying as fingernails on a blackboard. He hit the Off button with the heel of his hand then, after settling himself with a deep breath, crossed the room to her.

Arms folded beneath her breasts, her shoulders set, she showed him her back.

"I'm trying," he said carefully, "but I'll be damned if I can understand what this is about."

"It's about respect," she returned with a fierceness that set him back a full step when she spun around. "It's about recognizing me for my own strengths. For my own needs. It's about treating me like a woman."

He narrowed his eyes, wrestled with an uneasy and unsolicited flicker of anger. "I've always treated you like a woman."

"You've treated me like a piece of glass—like some porcelain doll you think you're going to break if you handle me too rough."

Confusion abetted frustration and drained him of the last of his patience. "My mistake for caring."

She shook her head and looked toward the ceiling. "I don't mean to make it sound like a bad thing. The way you treat me—it's…admirable."

"Admirable? My lovemaking is *admirable?*" Pride stole what loose grip he still held on reason. Sarcasm jumped in to break the contact completely. "Well, hell. Then my mission's accomplished. *Admirable* is exactly what I was shooting for."

Feeling like he was sinking in a quagmire of quicksand, he shoved his hands in his hip pockets and tried to settle himself down. "I thought I was making it good for you."

"It *is* good."

Her fluid softness confounded him even more.

"It's not just good. It's wonderful. It's wonderful, and sweet, and totally…controlled."

She gave, damn her, and then she took away. He was past frustration now and barreling toward just plain pissed. "I don't understand. I thought things were going so well. What is it you want from me?"

Emma knew she was handling this badly. She was doing exactly what she'd wanted to avoid doing. She was hurting him—blowing crater-sized holes through a highly vulnerable spot—the impenetrable James pride. But she couldn't stop now, not now that she'd mustered the courage to level with him.

"I need to make you understand something, Garrett. Something it took me a long time to understand myself. And I need you to listen—really listen to what I'm going to say. Now, more than ever, we need to make sure we're communicating."

"I thought we *were* communicating." He cast a dark look toward the loft. "I thought we were communicating just fine."

She let her breath out on a sigh. "If all it took to make this marriage work was you loving me and me loving you, we wouldn't be here, would we?"

She could not, Emma told herself, let guilt badger her out of finishing what she'd started. No matter how much the disclosures hurt him.

"Besides, *we* haven't been communicating. I have. *I've* been the one who's confided my heart's secrets to you. I've been the one who shared my feelings about my mother—confessed my sense of inadequacy and admitted to my fears."

She paused for a deep breath, fortifying herself as he scowled at her. "And yes, you've been supporting and loving and tolerant and wonderful, but you haven't come to terms with any of the issues that work on you."

"Issues? I don't know what you're talking about. I don't have any issues."

"Don't you?"

Silence crowded the cabin in thick, heavy layers.

"Talk to me, Garrett," she pleaded at last, her eyes and her voice letting him know she wasn't going to let him get by with denial or evasion any longer. "Talk to me or when we get back to Jackson, we go separate ways."

He looked at her like she'd cut his heart out. She wasn't so sure she hadn't sliced off a piece of hers, too.

"After what we've shared this week—after all we've been through, you'd still consider leaving me?"

She closed her eyes and looked away. "Garrett, with you in my life, there is purpose and power. The last thing I want to do is leave you. But no matter how much I love you, I can't live with you and not be your partner in every sense of the word."

He stared at her long and hard. "I swear, I don't know what you want from me."

"You do know. You just don't *want* to give it to me."

She rose from the chair, paced to the door. She ran a hand through her hair, then faced him again.

"Look. I know it goes against the grain. I know it's some man thing inside you that demands you must be silent and stoic and handle everything all by yourself. The sacred male credo. Be strong. Be invincible. Don't let 'em see you sweat, don't let 'em see you hurt.

"Only, I know better," she continued softly and went to him. "I know you hurt. I know when you're hurting—but you won't share it. And, Garrett, I can't stand it when you close yourself off and go through your pain alone. It's like twin slices from the same blade—I hurt because you're hurting, then I hurt because you won't let me help you. I can't stand it when you shut me out of your life that way."

She recognized his silence. It was the one that said he was fighting this, even though he knew she was making sense. ''All week I've tried to get you to talk to me, but you've proven you have no intention of doing that. Your mission, clearly, was to cater to my needs instead of yours. You took me horseback riding and hiking and looking for gold. You led me into conversations about Sara and about my mother and our concerns for her. But what did *you* talk about? Your brothers. Maya and Logan. We never talked about Garrett.''

He worked his jaw and glared over her head.

''God knows it isn't because I haven't tried to get you to. But every time I open a door for you to walk through and confide in me, you close it. Not with a slam, but with a gentle evasion, a tender smile, an impassioned kiss that led us away from your feelings and toward another disaster cloaked in play or lovemaking.''

''I wanted to make memories,'' he said defensively. ''I wanted to make love. I wanted to do everything two people in love are supposed to do.''

''Everything but talk about you and the hurts you harbor.''

He let out a weary breath.

''I need to understand, Garrett. I need to know how you feel about losing your father. How it made you feel to be a child yet be the oldest and feel like you have to carry the weight of your family on your shoulders. To always be the one everyone else turns to for answers and advice. To always feel like everyone is counting on you and that you can't afford the luxury of letting them down. Not once. Not even once—so you work harder and longer. I want to know why you won't cut yourself any slack, why you give to that business until you don't have anything left for yourself.''

''Back off,'' he snarled, so abruptly and with such anger her heart leaped to her throat.

''Why?'' she asked, almost afraid to, but knowing in her heart she'd struck a nerve so raw that exposing it was the only way to heal it.

''Why?'' she repeated more forcefully when his jaw clenched with the strain of his battle with control. ''Why, Garrett? Because I might find out the burden's been a little too heavy to bear?''

His stubborn silence reminded her of just how proud he was and how difficult this was for him. Because it was so difficult, she decided to ease off and try another tack.

''Garrett,'' she said gently and took his hand. With reluctance he let her lead him to the table where they sat down across from each other. ''I even feel you holding back when you make love to me. Even then, when you take me someplace beautiful, you hold back.''

His scowl was firm, his denial complete, when she covered his balled fists with her hands over the tabletop. ''I love how you touch me. I love how you know, even before I do, what I need, what I want. You give me everything a woman could ask for.

''You give me everything,'' she repeated softy. ''Everything but you. Don't you see? Even in bed you won't share what you feel, what you need with me. And what I need is all of you. Without restraint. Just now—out on the porch—you almost gave me that. And then you took it away.''

She saw the moment he understood. Recognized his argument even before he voiced it.

''I don't want to hurt you,'' he said darkly.

"Hurt me? How could you possibly hurt me when you're so busy protecting me?"

The words sounded brutal, even to her own ears. She tried to gentle them with the stroke of her fingers over his knuckles. "I know you don't mean to, but you hurt me every time you deny your own needs. You hurt me every time you treat me like some simpering Southern flower too delicate to handle the needs of a man."

"I don't treat you that way." His eyes were shadowed, his tone defensive. "I've never thought of you that way."

"Don't you?" she asked gently, trying to soften the sting of her words with the touch of her hands.

The muscle in his jaw knotted tight as he hung on to his resolve. "I try to take care with you."

"Yes. Yes, you do. And I love that about you. I love to be cared for by you. But sometimes I need more. Sometimes I need to know that you need me as much as I need you."

When his only response was a deep breath, she pressed on. "I need a partner, Garrett. A partner. Not a protector.

"That day," she continued, when her words had settled into an edgy silence. "The day I saw you with that woman—"

He rose so quickly his chair teetered as it scraped across the wooden floor with a serrated rasp. "I thought we'd gotten past that. How many times can I tell you, how many ways can I say it? I wasn't sleeping with her."

"I know." She followed him to where he stood at the back door. Stiff arms braced above his head on either side of the door frame, he stared broodily outside and into the night.

"I know that now," she repeated wanting to make sure he understood that she did.

"Then why are you bringing it up again?"

"Because you need to know what was going on with me then." And then came the really hard part. "You need to know how your holding back from me made me feel."

Nine

Emma watched the play of emotions shadow the rugged beauty of his face as he fixed his gaze on a spot in the darkness. He was closing up. He was closing off. His ego, his pride—she'd injured both badly—were at stake here. Recognizing that, understanding their importance to a man like him, she cautioned herself to go slow and easy, but to proceed no matter what the cost.

"Please don't close up on me now. You brought me here because you wanted to work this out. Garrett, there are layers upon layers of misunderstandings we have to work through if we're going to untangle all the knots. It's going to take both of us to do that. And if we can't get past this one, we don't have a chance of getting back to where we need to be."

She collected herself with a deep breath, then began again, picking up the threads of that tattered cloth he'd wanted to throw away.

"When I saw you with her, I saw you enjoying a woman who appeared to be everything I wasn't. She was aggressive, sophisticated, blatantly physical. All I could think was, this is what he wants? Someone he won't let me be?"

Clearly uncomfortable with her honesty, he lowered his chin to his chest, his silence as combative as any words. She couldn't let it stop her.

"So what did I do? Exactly what you expected. I played the part. I shattered like glass. All I saw was you with a strong, self-reliant woman—and I hated myself because she was everything I wasn't."

She closed her eyes. Rode out the pain that still crowded her from that day. "It was like a self-fulfilling prophecy. I'd become what I'd wanted to be for the man I'd wanted to be with and hadn't made allowances for what would happen if that man became bored with me. I felt like I'd driven you to her by being exactly what you wanted me to be. I was as angry with myself for being so malleable. I was angry with you for putting me in that position. And I couldn't think past it. I just reacted and decided to end it on my terms.

"That's when I started hating you. At least that's when I told myself I should hate you. Not only because I'd thought you'd betrayed me, but because you'd made me into what I was. Completely dependent, stupidly content to let you protect me from whatever it was you thought I couldn't handle.

"And superimposed over it all," she added, making herself go on, even though she knew her words were tearing him apart, "was the picture of my mother. Beaten. Broken. Living in a chemically fogged world and ignoring a husband who cheated on her without remorse because she felt that she'd failed. That she wasn't the woman he needed her to be. And, Garrett, I saw myself."

For a moment she was back there again. She was reliving that horrible day. "It shames me to admit it, but I actually thought about taking the same route she had. I had a full bottle of oblivion in my hand. I even thought about taking it a step further and ending it all."

"Jesus." His oath hissed out on a tortured breath.

As much as she was hurt for him, she made herself continue. "It was then that I knew I couldn't let this beat me. It was then I decided that if anyone was going to pay the price it was going to be you. Only we've both been paying ever since."

At the touch of her hand on his arm, he finally turned to her. The anguish in his eyes tore her apart.

"I'm sorry if hearing that hurt you. But if we're going to fix this, you have to know where I was, why I did what I did to you. It was knee-jerk. It was wrong. And I can never tell you how sorry I am."

He looked past her. Slowly methodically he collected himself. "Why didn't you come to me? I would have understood."

She shook her head, a sad smile tilting her lips. "Because you always understand. You would have said it's okay. Somehow you would have made me believe it. And that's as far as it would have gone. You would have shouldered the blame, shouldered the load, and made it go away for me. And that, Garrett, is a major part of our problem.

"For godsake, Em. How can there be a problem in understanding?"

"The problem is this way you have of being reasonable. Of being understanding to a fault. I never know what you're really thinking. I never know what your true feelings are because you're always so busy protecting me from them.''

"I thought that was part of loving you."

She shook her head. "So is leveling with me. I need that from you."

The breath he let out was weary, his patience clearly exhausted. "What is it that you want me to say?"

"What you feel," she ground out, her own frustration making her forget her bid to cater to his pride. "I want you to tell me what you really feel about what's happened between us. For starters you can tell me what you feel about what I did to you."

He roamed back to the table, slumped down in a chair.

"Garrett?"

With stiff, controlled movements, he lowered his face to his hands. "Don't push this, Em. I've taken all the hits I can for one night. Believe me, you don't want to hear what I feel."

"Why? Because it might hurt me? Because you might lose that precious control and say what you really want to say?"

He held his silence like a weapon.

"My God, Garrett—I drugged you. I shaved your head. I left you, accused you of adultery. You, a man who prides himself for his integrity, his sense of honor. You should hate me."

"You think I didn't want to?" For the first time his control cracked. He slammed his fist down on the table. His face was ravaged with rage and pain. "You think I haven't wanted to hate you for what you did—not only to me but to us? I've damned you a thousand times for the hell you put me through."

"But you fought it, didn't you?"

"I tried to understand," he said, each word measured in a bid to regain a handle on the patience he'd exhausted. "I tried to make some sense of it. And now you tell me that you don't want my understanding. You don't want me taking care—you don't want me caring about you. Apparently you never did."

He shoved up from the chair, radiating anger and fighting defeat. "I've loved you and only you since the first day I saw you, and I've never given you a reason to doubt that love. And yes, I wanted to hate you for what you did to me. But I kept loving you instead. And loving you means taking care of you. And yes, dammit, protecting you. Even if it's protecting you from me."

His eyes glittered in the shadowed room. His face was hard, yet achingly vulnerable.

"I give you everything I've got, Em. Everything I am. I don't know how to do it any other way. And now you tell me it's not enough."

He closed his eyes, drew in a deep draught of air. When he met her eyes, his were brimming with pain and despair and a helplessness bred by both. "What *is* enough, Em? What's it ever going to take to be enough for you?"

She didn't try to follow him when he shoved the door open and stalked outside. She didn't know what else to say. So she left him to the darkness and his anger and wearily climbed the stairs to the loft.

And then she prayed. She prayed for him. She prayed for herself. And she prayed that she hadn't just destroyed whatever hope they'd had of holding their marriage together.

The light by the bed cast a soft glow over the room when she turned it on, then lay down fully clothed.

Time crawled by in sluggish fragments that she marked by the slow slide of the moon across the sky.

By the time she heard the back door creak open and softly close, the first blush of dawn had stolen the edge from the night. Except for the violent pounding of her heart, silence settled again, until finally she heard the scuff of his boots cross the bare wood floor, the complaint of the loft stairs as they groaned beneath his ascending weight.

Curled on her side she watched him approach the bed. His face was haggard, his eyes weary as he crossed to the opposite side and sat, his back to her.

Shoulders hunched, he leaned forward, braced his forearms on his spread thighs. After a long moment, he glanced over his shoulder at her, then back to his loosely clasped hands.

"It's so big," he said finally, his words ragged, his admission complete. "This love I have for you. It's so big, sometimes it scares me. I didn't know, Em. I swear I didn't know what my holding back was doing to you."

He unclasped his hands, balled them into fists and braced stiff arms on the mattress on either side of his hips. "I've never known how to deal with it. I've never known how to let you in without making my hurt yours. Just like I've never known how to satisfy my needs without letting them take over."

He stared toward the ceiling. "A long time ago I decided the answer was to never let myself get out of control—emotionally or physically. That way I wouldn't take a chance on hurting you."

Finally he turned to her. "Tonight you made me realize it shouldn't have been up to me to make that choice. It should have been up to you."

He understood. Relief poured over her like a sunburst. It warmed the chill in her heart and eased the riot of doubt that had clogged her throat and made it difficult to breathe. Biting her lower lip to stall the threat of tears, she rose to her knees behind him.

Wrapping her arms around him, she lowered her cheek to his broad back. "All I've ever wanted—all I've ever needed—was to know you need me as much as I've always needed you."

He covered her hands with his, leaned back against her. "It never occurred to me that you didn't know that. Or that holding back would diminish how you felt about yourself."

"I just want to give back, Garrett. Please know…this is as much my fault as yours. I should have told you long ago. I didn't know how. You wouldn't let me in, you wouldn't let me help, so I turned away from you."

He twisted at the hip, lay back on the bed and took her down with him. "Turn to me now, Em," he whispered, searching her eyes as if he'd find the answer to all his questions there. "I need you to turn to me now."

More than love suffused his kiss, more than apologies softened his hold to a caress. He pressed her face to the hollow of his neck. "You're going to have to give me a little time to work with this though, okay?"

"Just let it happen," she murmured, and knew she was asking him to trust her to know not only what she needed from him but what he needed from her.

She pressed her lips to his throat where his pulse beat like thunder. And she waited.

Finally, after a long, decisive moment, he began to let it out. "It was my fault," he said out of the blue with an anguish so raw and riddled with guilt her heart stopped.

"What's your fault?" she whispered when she could

form the words. She touched a hand to his chest, felt the relentless crash of his heart beating beneath her palm. "What's your fault, Garrett?"

"It's my fault he's dead." He closed his eyes, turned away from her. "It's my fault my father is dead."

In her heart she'd suspected. In all these years of loving him, she'd suspected he had somehow held himself to blame. And yet, this was the first time he'd said the words aloud. The first time he'd shared the pain.

With gentle hands she turned him in her arms and drew him to her breast.

His arms came around her without hesitation as he buried his face between her breasts and held her like she was the only thing in the world he trusted to be his anchor.

"Tell me." She pressed her mouth to the top of his head. "Tell me."

It was difficult. More difficult than anything Garrett had ever done. But once he began talking, he couldn't seem to stop.

The words came like a flood, the disclosures swelling to the surface, crowding the banks of his silence, then spilling out onto the open field of endless, welcome relief.

And all the while, she listened. His wife. His lover. This woman whom he had taken to his heart and promised to protect, held him in her arms and bore the weight of his burdens on her slim shoulders.

"It was a Saturday," he said, letting out a breath that felt like it had been locked inside him for seventeen years. "I always helped him out on Saturdays. It was his way of letting me know he trusted me with some responsibility. His way of making some time for the two of us together. And it was my way of making some money. Something I never thought I had enough of back then.''

He nuzzled his face into her soft warmth, felt the strength and the steadiness of her heartbeat beneath his cheek. ''I'd been begging him to let me run the trencher. That day was the perfect opportunity. He was running a little behind schedule on the mall project. Needed to get the footings for the foundation dug so they could get the cement work done. I badgered. I wheedled. He finally relented.

''I really thought I was something,'' he continued and made himself go on. ''Riding that big machine. All that horsepower beneath me. All that power at my fingertips. And I was doing fine. I'd dug about fifteen yards when I caught sight of him. He was running toward me, waving his hands, shouting. I couldn't hear him above the roar of the machine. And it didn't register—not at first, anyway—that he was waving me off. I didn't realize it until later—after he'd jumped onto the trencher, shoved me off and onto the ground.''

A shudder rippled through him, unexpected, unstoppable. ''I was still rolling, spitting dust and wondering if the old man had gone crazy when I heard the explosion.''

He'd heard that roar a thousand times in his sleep. Felt the blast as the earth rumbled beneath him, the heat from the fire that blinded him as he'd stared in stunned horror at the burning inferno that had once been the trencher, with his father onboard.

''The machine had hit a gas main,'' he said, recounting the story he'd heard over and over again in the hours and days that followed. ''No one could figure out how Jonathan James—a man known for being meticulous and cautious to a fault—had missed the locator mark that had warned of the presence of the main.''

He felt her arms tighten around him. Beneath his cheek, her heart beat fast and hard. ''It wasn't him. It was me who hadn't recognized the significance of the orange arrow spray painted on the ground. It was me being macho and playing with power that cost him his life. And it's still me, all these years later, who has never told another living soul that I was driving the trencher that day.''

He stared thoughtfully into the misty light of morning. ''He gave his life for me. He shoved me off to save me and couldn't get the machine stopped in time to save himself.''

She understood now. She understood why his sense of responsibility stretched to the extreme. Why it was Garrett who had taken on the burden of man of the family. Why he had been the one to look out for his mother, for the business, for his brothers and why that had carried over to their marriage.

''You were a boy,'' she whispered against his hair. ''You were his pride and his reason for living, and what happened that day was a tragic, horrible accident. I won't, not even for a minute, try to deny you your sense of responsibility for it. I only ask that you accept that he never would have wanted you to blame yourself for his death.''

''I've tried,'' he uttered, his words heavy with the weight of the burden he'd taken upon himself to bear, ''every day of my life I've tried to make it up to him. I've tried to make it up to my mother and my brothers.''

''And you're tired,'' she said softly, soothingly. ''And you don't have to handle it all by yourself anymore.''

"I need you, Em. I need you so bad."

"I'm here," she whispered. "I've always been here."

She rocked him like a child. Stroked her hand over his hair. Hugged him to her breast. And finally, after all those years of holding it in, she let her own tears fall as he cried for the boy who had lost his father, as he mourned for the man who was responsible for his death.

His silent tears fell warm on her breast long after sleep—numbing, healing, necessary—finally claimed him. With him still wrapped snugly in her arms, she let it take her, too.

Hours later she awoke alone. Sunlight slanted through the windows, glinted off the walls, telling her it was late morning, possibly close to noon. She rose, walked downstairs and found him outside, down by the river.

She went to him, snuggled close to his side when he raised his arm and made a place for her there.

For a long moment Garrett stared out over the river in a silence that was both peaceful and healing. The disclosures had been painful for him. The truths, revealing.

In the past few hours he'd come to grips with the fact that he had been pouring more of his energy into the construction business his father left in his keeping than he had into their marriage. His self-blame had driven him to make the business so successful that he had sacrificed time with Emma and Sara. His closing that part of himself off from her had contributed to her sense of distrust.

Thanks to her, he'd come to terms with the damage he'd done. By suppressing his emotions, he had unintentionally distanced himself from her, instilled her with her own feelings of loss and failure.

The truth had been hard for him to face. In fact, he still hurt from the telling and the conclusions. But a monumental weight had been lifted, and he recognized now that his silence and his reluctance to share had been the factor that had driven them apart. She'd known all along what had taken him this long to accept.

"How did I ever get so lucky to have you in my life? And why wasn't I smart enough to realize how strong you really are?"

"I'm strong because of you. And together we have enough strength to move mountains."

He turned her in his arms. "I didn't think it was possible to love you more. But I do, Em. I'm falling in love with you all over again."

"I've never stopped loving you. I'll never stop loving you. And I never wanted to leave you. Never."

They were words he longed to hear. They were words he'd missed for so long.

She pressed her cheek to his chest. "Let's have another baby."

He hadn't been prepared for her request or the avalanche of feelings that followed. He tried not to, but he stiffened.

"Don't," she warned, reading his reaction for what it was. "Don't close off from me now, not now that we've gotten this far. It's been two years since the miscarriage. It's time we think about it. It's time we talk about it."

He took a deep breath. Rolled his shoulders and made himself relax. The next words out of her mouth brought home how important this was to her—to both of them.

"This is one more discussion we've avoided for too long."

With brutal honesty he realized that for the first time he completely understood what she'd been trying to tell him. She needed to know his thoughts. And he needed to share them. It was a new kind of honesty for him. One that was founded in trust. And it was crucial for a renewed beginning with the woman with whom he shared a daughter and a history too rich to discard for the sake of his pride.

For long moments they sifted through that horrible time in silence. She'd been so excited about the baby. A boy. They'd been trying for so long. The miscarriage had been devastating. The fact that he'd been out of town on a business trip and she'd had to handle it alone had been hard on both of them.

"You were so broken," he said into the silence. "I didn't know what to do. I didn't know how to help you."

"I know. And you tried. You held me when I cried. And I was too weak, both physically and emotionally to tell you how much losing the baby hurt. Even though I knew we both needed to talk about it. Even though I knew you thought you were sparing me."

She was right. Again. They had needed to talk about it then as much as they needed to talk about it now. He'd been wrong to keep his silence and encourage hers. He understood now how that tactic had added weight to the guilt. Her next words voiced his exact thoughts.

"We can't go on thinking for each other, Garrett. We have to ask. We have to agree to tell. We have to hash out the hurts and not think we're protecting each other by keeping our feelings inside."

He wrapped his arms around her. "I wanted the baby so badly. I hated myself for being gone and leaving you to deal with it alone."

"And you blamed yourself."

"Yes," he admitted. "I figured that somehow it had to be my fault."

"Are we past that now? Can you promise me that you'll stop punishing yourself by assuming the guilt for everything that goes wrong in our lives?"

He smiled grimly. "I can promise that I'll try. And I'll start with asking, how long have you been thinking about a baby?"

"Almost since we lost him." And then she made an admission of her own. "But I thought you didn't want to, because maybe you blamed me and didn't trust me to carry another child."

He groaned and swore under his breath.

"I know now that wasn't true. But that's what silence does. It creates distance. It lets in doubt and breeds assumptions—like the one I drew when I saw you with that woman. It had been two years and I was still feeling grief and inadequacy over losing the baby. I translated it into inadequacy as a wife."

He crushed her in his arms. "All that's over now. That, I promise with all my heart. You want a baby? I can't think of anything that would make me happier than having another baby with you.

"I want you as my wife, Emma. I want you as my lover. As my confidante—and most important, as my partner. With everything I have, I promise I'll trust you to be the keeper of my heart, my secrets and my soul. I'll trust you to let me be weak and let me be strong."

"I'll let you be anything you want to be," she whispered as a tear trailed down her cheek, "as long as you let me be there for you."

He kissed her. Sweetly. Deeply.

"Come on," he urged and, taking her hand, led her back toward the cabin. "Let's go make a baby."

He fed her first. And because they were both exhausted from the emotional release of the morning, they made sweet, slow love and fell immediately asleep.

Dusk was creeping across the western horizon when Emma felt Garrett stir and stretch and slowly come awake. She worked fast to tighten the last knot.

By the time he opened his eyes, she was feeling a little uneasy and wondering if her methods had crossed the line to extreme.

His eyes were blurry, a little out of focus, with the look of a man well loved.

He smiled, all sleepy and sexy when he spotted her kneeling naked on the bed beside him. Then he reached for her—at least he tried to.

His confusion lasted long enough to feed her guilt before he twisted his head around and discovered she'd bound his wrists to the headboard of the bed.

He tested the knots she'd made from pieces of lingerie, then gave her a long, questioning look. Finally a slow, wicked grin tilted one corner of his mouth. "And me without my video camera," he murmured with a thoroughly staged and wholly decadent leer.

She shot him a nervous smile, kissed him lightly on the cheek then crawled off the bed.

"And just where do you think you're going?"

His question was more curious than threatening, but she tensed anyway.

"Not far," she promised as she pulled the sheet up to his waist then began to gather her clothes.

Clearly baffled now, he just watched her, his expression guarded.

"Comfy?" she asked as she zipped up her jeans and tugged a sweater over her head.

He nodded then watched with an increasingly confounded frown when she checked her knots.

"Not too tight? Circulation okay?"

His eyes never left hers as he flexed his fingers, the action reflexive, automatic. "Fine. Em—what's going on?"

"In a minute." She crossed the room, dragged a brush through her hair, then came back to sit beside him. "Are you thirsty? Would you like some coffee or some water?"

He let go of a nervous chuckle. "What I'd like is an explanation. Would you mind telling me what this is about?"

"It's about trust," she began as she laced her fingers together on her lap. "It's about the fact that now that we've opened up this new line of communication, I'm going to make sure we keep it open."

His frown upgraded to a puzzled scowl. "And you think you have to tie me to the bed to do that?"

"No," she said a little shyly, then let a smile—sexy, seductive and ripe with a sense of awakening power—tilt her lips. "I think this is something I just want to do."

He had nothing to say to that—which was fine with her for the moment because she had plenty of things just bursting to be said and done—if she didn't lose her nerve.

"This," she said, touching her fingertips to his wrist,

then running them in a slow, intimate caress down his bare forearm, across his exposed armpits to rest on his chest, "this is our final moment of truth, Garrett."

She felt his big body tense, then shiver with an elemental rush of desire.

"Moment of truth?" he managed as she gave his other arm the same sensual, erotic attention as she had the other. "I'd...have bet the farm we've had several moments of truth the past few hours...some of them in this bed."

He swallowed back a groan when she trailed her fingers through his chest hair then drew a circle around his navel with one single, silky glide of her index finger.

"You're right," she agreed, a secret smile tilting her lips when his abdominal muscles clenched beneath her touch. "We did. And this is the last one. The last step to complete and total trust."

Watching his face, seeing the fire spark his eyes to blue flames, she reached for him then cupped and stroked his sex beneath the concealing sheet.

He shuddered and arched and instantly swelled into her kneading hand.

"So—" he caught his breath, rode with her touch "—this would be another one of those layers you were talking about."

She nodded at his acknowledgment, then slowly tugged the sheet aside until he was naked and completely vulnerable to whatever it was she wanted to do to him.

"Be gentle with me," he murmured as a slow, sexy smile crawled up his beautiful face. "It's my first time."

Ten

His smile was a decoy. They both knew that. He was still unsure about this. This man, who had held himself in check for so long, didn't know if he could allow himself to let go.

Emma didn't give him the option.

And it wasn't gentle. It couldn't have been. He was too needy. And she—she was a woman with one mission in mind.

Making sure she had his complete attention, she rose and slowly undressed for him.

Garrett watched, knowing she wanted him to, knowing he couldn't have torn his eyes away if he'd been pressed to at gunpoint.

He knew where the power was then. So did she. And she used it. To make him want. To make him need. To drive him to that jagged edge where surrender transcended to power and control broke down to pure, unbridled greed.

Dusky light limned her body in gold. Her hair fell across one side of her face in silken waves. Her eyes were dark as she came to him, a little dangerous, unabashedly daring. Her hands were restless, as was her touch, as she pressed her body against his with the same evocative boldness as she'd undressed for him.

And her sweet mouth was open and wanton and lush, as she bent to him, tasted the essence of him, surrounded him in velvet heat.

He groaned her name, and with one hard, vicious yank, broke the silken ties that bound him. It took everything in him to keep from taking the control she was so bent on testing.

But taking control and losing it were twin edges of a jagged blade. If he took control, he'd diminish hers. If he lost control, as she wanted him to, he might hurt her.

He chose the middle road, contented himself with touching her, knotting his hands in her hair—then sank into excruciatingly exquisite despair when she began her seduction in earnest.

She was fragrant heat, essentially woman. Her bold possession shot him to flash point so swiftly the blood left his head in a dizzying rush. What was left of his reason quickly followed.

Then all there was was sensation—and a wild craving that gave the caged beast in him a dangerous taste of freedom.

When she lifted her head, she left him hungry. She left him hot. His fists in her hair tightened, held, demanded what he would have never before dared to take. But she had another end in mind for him as she denied his clench-jawed plea and freed herself from the hands that begged her.

She rose above him—an erotic, pagan priestess—and made him a supplicant at her altar.

He'd never wanted this badly. He'd never needed this much. It was primitive and potent—and she fed the desire with bite-sized pieces when he wanted to tear into it with his teeth.

She knelt above him, over him, tormenting him with the brazen touch of her hands to her breasts until he reared up and took her in his mouth. He wasn't tender. He wasn't anything but what she'd tempted him to be: selfish, ravenous, he suckled and feasted and gorged himself on a need that only she could satisfy and he could no longer control.

Only it wasn't enough. It would never be enough until she was covering him, surrounding him, sheathing him inside her.

Restraint became an abstract, distant fallacy as she tormented him with the suggestive brush of her body over his.

A growl, guttural and savagely fierce, rumbled from somewhere deep in his gut as he clutched her hips in his hands and demanded she take him inside.

With hungry hands she surrounded him. With a siren's smile she guided him home—on her terms, in her own time—and took him deep.

Sin had never been this seductive. The claw of lust never as ravaging, as he lifted his hips and begged her to ride with him past the boundaries of love and into an unknown realm of passion.

He was soaring. She was the sky. He was the lightning unleashed and unrepentant in the rage of the storm she'd conjured. Utterly consumed, completely vulnerable, he let the thunder take him.

He couldn't plunge deep enough, couldn't get close enough as he pumped into her, harder, faster, then rode with her to the pulsing edge of release—and to an end as stunning as death, as sharply thrilling as escaping it.

Sleep claimed him again like a drug. Peace filled him like fine whiskey, a mellow burn, a warm, satisfying contentment. And when he awoke, hours later, it was to morning light and the provocative sight of his wife standing on the other side of the loft.

To the muffled creak of the old oak bed frame, the soft rustle of smooth sheets, he rolled to his side to better enjoy the view. Her back to him, wearing only the shirt he'd discarded when they'd gone to bed, she stood studying the pictures on the wall. When she reached above her head to straighten one of the framed prints, the luscious curve of her bare bottom peeked out from under the hem of his shirt.

"I guess," he said lazily, breaking the quiet and causing her to jump and press a hand to her throat in surprise, "if I had to wake up to an empty bed, this is the next best thing."

It took her a moment to catch her breath. "I was trying not to wake you."

"Well, I'm awake now, sunshine. And I want you to come here."

He tossed back the covers. Levering himself up on an elbow, he patted the mattress in front of him. Her gaze tracked his naked length with a lover's intimacy, lingering on that part of him that was swollen and straining for want of her.

"Now," he said darkly.

She walked toward him, a smug, sexy smile tilting her lips. As one, their thoughts returned to last night and the urgency with which he'd taken her, the freedom he'd allowed himself in the taking.

She lowered a knee to the bed. "I think I woke up a sleeping lion."

He trailed his hand up the inside of her thigh, sucked in a breath when she trembled. "Take it off."

Her eyes darkened then fired as she undid the buttons, shrugged his shirt from her shoulders and let it fall, forgotten, to the floor.

"I don't think I can walk." In fact, he was surprised he had the strength to talk.

Spread-eagle on his back, his breath slogged out in deep, labored puffs. On her stomach beside him, Emma balled a pillow under her breasts, hugged it to her cheek and grinned at him. "Sooner or later we're going to have to put it to the test."

"Later," he grunted, stalled somewhere between ecstasy and exhaustion. "Definitely later."

She laughed, a rich, throaty chuckle. "I love you this way."

"Half-dead?"

"Wholly satisfied. Totally spent. Completely at my mercy."

Serious suddenly, he held her gaze. "Thank you, Em. Thank you for showing me. Not just the sex. For everything."

"You're very welcome," she whispered, then with a teasing light returning to her eyes, trailed her fingers across his chest, and lower.

He caught her hand with a groan. "You're going to kill me."

"Not what I had in mind." She sat up cross-legged in the middle of the bed. "I've still got use for you, partner, so how about if I feed you to get your strength built back up?"

"A half a beef ought to do it."

She rose with a laugh, wholly confident, lavishly female, and shrugged into his shirt again. "Think you can make do with steak and eggs?"

The thought of all that silky skin beneath the coarse chambray of his shirt had his blood running hot again. "And then?"

"And then," she purred huskily and lowered her mouth for one last kiss, "you're going to take me treasure hunting."

"Again?"

"Again. It's our last day. We've got to give it one more try."

"So this has nothing to do with me," he teased, falling back on the bed and working hard to look wounded. "It's Frank and Jesse's gold you're after."

"Oldest motive known to man—or woman," she added with a sassy grin. "And that reminds me—" barefoot, she crossed the room to the picture "—this is of them, isn't it?"

"Yeah." He rolled to his side, content to just look at her. "It's an old tintype Dad discovered, had blown up and framed."

"There's a striking resemblance to you boys."

"So we've been told," he said dryly.

"When was it taken, do you think?"

"Shortly before they were run out of the valley. Story goes that it was the photographer in Jackson Hole who recognized them and alerted the local sheriff, who put

the word out to the officials in Arkansas who were looking for them.''

She studied the picture a little longer. ''Which one is
Frank?''

''The mean-looking one. Jesse was the baby—had
the baby face to go with it, too. Just like our Jess.
You're awfully interested in them all of a sudden.''

She worked her lower lip with her teeth, nodded.
''Have you ever noticed this—whatever it is—hanging
around Frank's neck?''

He shrugged. ''Hadn't paid much attention.''

''It looks like a strip of leather with a piece of wood
or something attached to it.'' Her brow furrowed. ''Wait
a minute. You know those things you showed me the
other day?'' At his blank look, she elaborated. ''You
know—the gun barrel, the hinge, those shell casings
you found when you were kids?''

''Yeah…I remember.''

''Well, this thing…this thing around his neck. It
looks kind of like one of those shell casings.''

His interest piqued, he rose, found he could walk after all and joined her by the picture. ''You're right. It
does look like a spent shell.''

''Why do you suppose he'd wear something like that
around his neck?''

He lowered his mouth to the curve of her neck, nuzzled lingeringly, his mind turning to other things.
''Maybe it was a souvenir. Something to remind him of
a particular job they'd pulled. Who knows how a crim-
inal mind works.'' He tugged her back against him.
''Wanna know how my mind is working right now?''

She leaned into his caress, laughed. ''No question
there. At this particular moment, you're as easy to read
as a primer.''

She turned in his arms. "But you need nourishment, remember? And I could use a shower."

"Good idea." His grin was lascivious and completely without shame. "I'll wash your back—and any other little thing that needs attention."

Their late breakfast turned into a very late brunch—and with the heat of this newfound passion in their relationship once again cooled, they both started thinking about the picture of the James boys and the possibility that there was some significance to the shell casing Frank had worn.

They both looked toward the old pine chest and the drawer that held the James boys' childhood finds with the same questions in their minds.

Fifteen minutes later, an effervescent excitement bubbled through their blood like fine champagne as Garrett held one of the brass shell casings between his fingers. There were five casings in all. Four of them were hollow and empty. The fifth had been sealed at both ends. The letters *F.J.* had been crudely carved on the scarred three-inch-long brass outer shell.

Attention focused and intent, Emma watched over Garrett's shoulder. "Can you get it open?"

He'd been carefully working the end with pliers, trying to pop the seal free. "I need something smaller, something sharper to wedge between the casing and the seal."

"A hair clip?" she suggested as she pulled the gold barrette from her hair.

"Yeah, that just might work."

With the precision of a jeweler, he worked the sharp edge of the fastener in between the fused metals. After several minutes, it broke free with a surprising pop and tumbled onto the table.

"I'll be damned." He scowled into the dark cylinder that wasn't quite as big around as his index finger. "There's something in there. I can't get it out."

"Let me try."

Emma took the casing, gingerly stuck her pinkie in up to the first joint and with a little careful manipulation, managed to pull its contents free.

With excited eyes, they stared at a tiny rolled cylinder of dried, brittle paper.

"Holy horse thief, Robin," Garrett said, in his best Batman voice. "I think we've got a breakthrough."

Anticipation added a charged edge to her excitement. "Unroll it. See what it says."

"I'm afraid to—it's so brittle, it might break into dust."

"Let's try a little steam to soften it up," she suggested and hurried to put the teakettle on to boil.

Fifteen minutes later they stared in intrigued silence at the letters scrawled on the paper they'd managed to unroll. Some were indecipherable, the ink was so faded. Some appeared to be destroyed by the cracks in the aged paper.

"I can make out about every other letter on the top line. There's a *W* and an *I*. And I think that's a *K*. Damn, it's just too hard to read."

Emma added an *S* and a *Y* until, in order, they read *W-I-S-K-Y*. The second line, though smudged, appeared to be intact: *R-I-S*.

"What do you think it means?"

He shrugged, slumped back in the chair. "I don't know. Could be a code of some kind. Maybe a combination to some vault. *W-I-S-K-Y*. *R-I-S*," he repeated aloud letter by letter. Together they tried to construct a word or a phrase or a name. Finally he shook his head. "It's like playing poker with half a deck. The closest I can come up with is he was a bad speller and was trying to write *whiskey* and *rice*. Maybe it was a list of supplies he needed."

She studied it closer. "It's got to mean something. It's got to be important for Frank to have worn it around his neck."

"Woah. You've jumped from speculation to fact pretty fast there, girl. We don't even know for certain if this is the shell in the picture."

"What else could it be?"

While he was hard-pressed to discourage her, he couldn't make the shift from speculation to fact as easily as she. "Okay. Let's say it is. It still looks to me like it's of no more significance than a grocery list."

She didn't give his theory any more import than a quick roll of her eyes before another thought stopped her. "I wonder how it ended up here."

"Well." He could only speculate. "We found the shells scattered along the river—close to the spot you found the gold coin—maybe he took it off to take a bath. Maybe he got caught without it when the law showed up and chased his outlaw butt back to Arkansas."

"That happened? It happened here—in the valley?"

"So the story goes."

Caught up in the excitement, she sat down at the table beside him. "I think I want to hear the whole story."

"It's just a story, remember that," he cautioned, then proceeded to tell her what his father had told him.

"Supposedly Frank and Jesse had decided to hold their last job—the one that netted them the chest of gold—and had taken off for Wind River to hide out for a while before heading to California and a life of luxury.

"Supposedly," he repeated, reemphasizing that what he was telling her could just as well be fiction as fact, "they figured no one would look for them this far west, so they got comfortable here. A little too comfortable. They forgot to watch their backs. And as I mentioned before, they actually had their picture taken—which ended up being their downfall.

"When the posse came several months later, they caught them flat-footed. The boys only had time to saddle up and get out of Dodge, leaving everything—including the gold—behind."

She touched a finger to the paper. "This is significant," she said decisively, after listening with rapt attention. "Frank must have written it down, tucked it in the shell, then strung it around his neck so he'd have a record of how to find the gold if they ever got separated from it. They were killed before they could get back here.

"I can feel it, Garrett." She was so excited she was bouncing in the chair. "Why else would Frank have worn the shell around his neck, and what else could this really be?" Carefully straightening the paper, she studied the cryptic message again.

He leaned his chin in the cup of his palm and watched her. "You look really cute when you get greedy, did you know that?"

Her grin was wicked and determined. "And you look just like an outlaw on horseback."

He cocked a brow. "That's a hint, right?"

"Saddle up, Garrett James, we've got a treasure to hunt."

* * *

It came to her like the proverbial bolt out of the blue. They'd been wandering the river's edge, enjoying the sun and the fun and each other when she stopped short and grabbed his hand.

"It wasn't an *I*. It was an *O*. And it wasn't an *S*. It was a *K*."

Garrett stared at her like she'd arrived by spaceship. "What?"

"The note. It was an *O*, only part of it was smeared. And it wasn't an *S*. It's another *K*. Not *R I S*, but *R O K*. *W I S K Y. R O K*. Whiskey Rock!"

"So he couldn't spell. It still means nothing."

"It means everything," she insisted and pointed straight ahead. "Look. The rock. The one that looks like a bottle. The one you boys carved your initials on. It reminded Frank of a bottle, too—a rock that looked like a whiskey bottle. Whiskey rock. That rock is the clue to where he hid the gold."

Garrett narrowed his eyes, studied the rock, studied her. "It's a stretch," he said finally, then quickly added when she scowled, "but, I'll go along with the possibility."

"Possibility, my butt—"

He swung her around and, laughing at the strength of her conviction, caught the part of her anatomy in question in his big hands. "And a sweet one it is, too."

She made a halfhearted struggle before succumbing to the smile in his eyes and the persuasion of his kiss.

"Is finding the gold really that important to you?"

Emma had never been into symbolism, but suddenly she was certain that the gold stood for more than the whisper of a legend. It was symbolic of their love. Eternal. Enduring. And no, finding the gold wasn't important. Finding their love and the means to keep it was.

She framed his face in her hands. "You're what's important to me."

"I brought the blanket," he whispered against her mouth.

Whipping his hat from his head and settling it on hers, she snuggled closer. "By all means, you should be rewarded for your foresight."

He lifted her into his arms, carried her to the blanket and laid her down. "I love you, Em. I'll always love you."

On a far ridge, two riders reined in their mounts and surveyed the valley below them.

"What do you think?" Jesse asked as he leaned a forearm on the saddle horn. "Is it safe to go down there?"

Clay lowered the binoculars. He scratched his head and fought a grin as his big bay gelding shifted beneath him. "Not just yet. Let's give 'em another half hour and then make our move."

Jesse snorted impatiently. "They've been here for seven days. What's another half hour going to accomplish?"

"The difference," Clay said, sounding wise beyond his years and enjoying the fact that his smug grin was irritating the hell out of his younger brother. "All the difference in the world."

With Clay and Jesse in the lead and Emma and Garrett riding double and pulling up the rear, the four riders left the Wind River retreat a few hours later.

Garrett reined in as they crested the ridge. Together he and Emma looked down over the valley.

"Does it bother you that we left without the infamous James Gang gold?"

She snuggled against him. "I'm content to pass on the torch to your brothers."

In his wife's eyes, Garrett saw that her thoughts echoed his. What they were taking with them from the valley was far more valuable than gold: the sweet and perfect knowledge that from this day forward, the love they had renewed would be as enduring as the river, as lasting as the memories they had made in this special place.

"Let's go home," he said, and nudged the mare with his knees.

Emma took one last, lingering look over the valley. She wouldn't have missed this past week for anything in the world. But she missed their daughter. She missed their life.

"Yes," she agreed, turning toward the other side of the mountain. "It's time to go home."

* * * * *

Take 2 bestselling love stories FREE

Plus get a FREE surprise gift!

Special Limited-Time Offer

Mail to Silhouette Reader Service™

3010 Walden Avenue
P.O. Box 1867
Buffalo, N.Y. 14240-1867

YES! Please send me 2 free Silhouette Desire® novels and my free surprise gift. Then send me 6 brand-new novels every month, which I will receive months before they appear in bookstores. Bill me at the low price of $3.12 each plus 25¢ delivery and applicable sales tax, if any.* That's the complete price, and a saving of over 10% off the cover prices—quite a bargain! I understand that accepting the books and gift places me under no obligation ever to buy any books. I can always return a shipment and cancel at any time. Even if I never buy another book from Silhouette, the 2 free books and the surprise gift are mine to keep forever.

225 SEN CH7U

Name	(PLEASE PRINT)	
Address	Apt. No.	
City	State	Zip

This offer is limited to one order per household and not valid to present Silhouette Desire® subscribers. *Terms and prices are subject to change without notice.
Sales tax applicable in N.Y.

UDES-98   ©1990 Harlequin Enterprises Limited

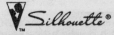

COMING NEXT MONTH

#1177 SLOW TALKIN' TEXAN—Mary Lynn Baxter
Ornery Porter Wyman, November's *Man of the Month*, was married to his Texas fortune, but money couldn't mother his baby boy. Sexy, nurturing Ellen Saxton...now, *she* could raise a child. *And* this single father's desire...for marriage?

#1178 HER HOLIDAY SECRET—Jennifer Greene
Her past twenty-four hours were a total blank! By helping elusive beauty Maggie Fletcher regain her lost day, small-town sheriff Andy Gautier was in danger of losing his *bachelorhood*. But would Maggie's holiday secret prevent her from becoming this lawman's Christmas bride?

#1179 THIRTY-DAY FIANCÉ—Leanne Banks
The Rulebreakers
Tough-as-nails Nick Nolan was lovely Olivia Polnecek's childhood protector. Now *she* was coming to *his* rescue by posing as his fiancée. She'd always dreamed of wearing Nick's ring, sleeping in his arms. So playing "devoted" was easy—and all part of her plan to turn their thirty-day engagement into a thirty-*year* marriage....

#1180 THE OLDEST LIVING MARRIED VIRGIN—
Maureen Child
The Bachelor Battalion

When innocent Donna Candello was caught tangled in Jack Harris's bedsheets, the honorable marine married her in name only. But their compromising position hadn't actually *compromised* Donna Candello at all...and the oldest living married virgin's first wedded task was to convince her new husband to give his blushing bride somethin' to *blush* about!

#1181 THE RE-ENLISTED GROOM—Amy J. Fetzer
Seven years ago levelheaded Maxie Parrish shocked rough-'n'-reckless Sergeant Kyle Hayden, leaving *him* at the altar. And nine months later Maxie had a surprise of her own! Now a certain never-forgotten ex-fiancé appeared at Maxie's ranch rarin' to round up the wife that got away...but what of the daughter he never knew?

#1182 THE FORBIDDEN BRIDE-TO-BE—Kathryn Taylor
Handsome, wealthy Alex Sinclair was Sophie Anders's perfect marriage match. Problem was, she already had a fiancé—his brother! True, her engagement was a phony, but the baby she was carrying was for real—and belonged to Alex. Once Sophie began to "show," would Alex make their forbidden affair into a wedded forever after?